I0727780

Weave: Rapunzel Retold

DEMELZA CARLTON

A tale in the Romance a Medieval Fairy Tale series

Some kings were as immovable as granite. Others appeared as firm as permafrost, but melted at the first breath of spring breeze, hinting at the good fortune to come. And some drooled like hunting hounds at the slightest whiff of scraps from her table.

King Thorn was definitely a dog. So gullibly parted from his gold, Kun almost felt guilty about it. Almost.

So when he sent word that he wished an audience with Mistress Kun, she did not make him wait long. She waited until he was seated on his throne before the court, and cast a portal right in the middle of his great hall. No one could say she didn't make an entrance.

Gasps and screams greeted her. Even Thorn himself rose from his seat with fear on his face, if only for a moment, before he remembered he had an audience. Then he was every inch the king again.

Kun swirled her cape about her. She quite liked this one – black with several layers to it, so it looked like a flock of ravens taking flight when she tossed it just right. Rapunzel had outdone herself on it.

"You wanted a witch, Your Majesty?" she asked, not bothering to bow. She'd only ever bowed to one king, and she would never do so again.

"You!"

She could hear the courtiers behind her, muttering and murmuring, but she paid them no attention. The only words she cared to hear were the ones where Thorn told her what he wanted, so that she might name her price. So she stayed silent, and waited. The eager hound had never practiced patience.

"Did you not promise me that the merchant's daughter, Lady Zuleika, would give me an heir to the throne?" Thorn thundered.

"Indeed I did." It was the easiest gold she'd ever made, for she'd already known the girl was pregnant. Her son was on Beacon Isle even now, thriving.

"So before all my court, tell me…where is my heir?"

She folded her arms across her chest. "On Beacon Isle, with his mother, of course. The safest place in the kingdom to keep a crown prince."

More gasps from the crowd. Ah, they had not known about the child, either. Well, it was no secret that Thorn was not on good terms with his brother, the Master of Beacon Isle. But not to know that Vardan and his wife had borne a son…

"You lie!" Thorn roared.

"You have only to go to Beacon Isle yourself to see the child, if you do not believe me. For the next King of Aros is there, though he is still but a babe." Kun fixed her gaze on the king. "Surely you do not fear the Master of Beacon Isle, Your Majesty. He is, after all, your brother. I'm sure he would welcome you with open arms."

Well, perhaps he would, if there wasn't the matter of that cursed mirror, and the things Thorn had done to Vardan's wife…

Who had been terribly clever with her revenge, to Kun's chagrin. If Zuleika had actually cursed King Thorn instead of casting a curse that only activated if he harmed her, and actually warning him about it…no, Kun could not blame the girl for Thorn's fate. But if she had…then Kun would have been justified in binding the young enchantress as a djinn. With both Zuleika and Rapunzel, no one would have been able to stand against her and her mission.

Even if she'd still had Briska, it would have been better, but that damned genie had managed to free himself from the lamp and steal Briska from her, too.

But instead of thinking about all those other people who might have been there to help her, Kun should have been listening to Thorn.

"I declare you guilty, traitor, and your sentence is death!" Thorn announced.

Wait…what?

Thorn drew his sword. "Kneel, traitor."

"Oh, you can't be serious," Kun said, and turned on her heel to leave.

She bit her thumb, using the blood to draw a circle in the air until a portal appeared.

Searing pain lanced through her chest.

Kun blinked. Was that a sword in front of her? That couldn't be right. It was all bloody, like it had gone right through…right through…

She tumbled through the portal, sliding off the blade, barely feeling when her unconscious body hit the flagstones.

"Mother! Mother!" Rapunzel screamed.

Through the portal, she could still see the triumphant king, standing with his bloodied sword.

"You don't deserve that crown, Thorn," Rapunzel spat before the portal closed.

Then she did her best to make her unconscious godmother comfortable as she took her final, bubbling breath.

Two

Isaak stood on the riverbank, dwarfed by the enormous waterwheel that stood unusually still. "You summoned me, Your Majesty?"

Rosaline had told him that most queens spent their days sewing or weaving in their chambers, only occasionally riding out for hawking or hunting if they fancied such sports. But Queen Molina was not most queens, as she sloshed through the hip-deep water in the millrace, with her skirts kilted up past her knees.

"You're a Master Artificer now. You and Romein. What do you make of this mill wheel? Can you tell me why it has stopped?" she asked.

Isaak tugged off his boots and jumped into the millrace beside his queen, careful not to splash her. "The water flow is not enough to make it turn. The water levels are too low, and the wheel is large and heavy. Perhaps when the autumn rains begin, and the water levels in the river rise, the wheel will turn again."

Queen Molina nodded. "If we could but wait for summer's sluggish flows to speed up in autumn, your reasoning would be sound. But this is the city's water supply, and the canals cannot run dry. The wheel must turn, and water must flow. How would you harness the sluggish summertime river to serve the city's needs?"

Isaak considered for a moment. "Perhaps a smaller wheel…" He shook his head. "It is this wheel that must turn, to supply the city. So a smaller wheel in its place would not do. But an additional small wheel, one which will turn in the summer current, yet big enough to fill the millrace so that the larger wheel might turn…"

Molina clapped her hands. "And this is why I tell Lubos I need more apprentices! I cannot do everything, or even think of everything, and the more bright minds we have in the kingdom, the more they can learn, and take it out to the rest of the country…and beyond!'

Isaak's ears pricked up. "You would have me undertake a quest for you, Your Majesty?"

Molina sighed. "If I had my way, I would send you to take up your father's lands, to rule them as he did before he turned traitor. The steward does a fine job of sending in the tithes, but he will hear none of my plans for waterwheels at Burg Rumpelstiltskin. Yet the river there is perfect year round – you could have wheels on both sides of the castle, and run more than one mill! And yet…" She clenched her calloused hands into fists. "The world changes every day, and only fools delude themselves that things can stay the same. Today, you are young and strong with the kind of cleverness our kingdom sorely needs. Yet tomorrow, you might succumb to your father's curse."

Isaak closed his eyes. He'd heard the story a thousand times, so it should have lost the ability to frighten him, yet it still sent a chill through his heart.

"Yes, my queen. Tomorrow, I may wake up and everything I touch turns to gold, and on that day, I will have only a year left to live. If I inherited my father's curse, which you told me he insisted only you could save me from. And you have saved me. I have been a ward of the crown ever since the king's father died, and my father disappeared. Is it not too much to hope for that you have saved me from my father's fate as well?" Isaak asked.

Molina sighed again. She did not share his hope. "Come to my bower. I have something to show you. Something I should have given you years ago, but…Lubos said you were too young. But now you are a man grown, you deserve to choose your own path. Wherever it may lead."

She led the way across the bailey and into the castle, heedless of the water dripping from her skirts along the flagstones. "Send for some ale from the kitchens while I change out of my wet things," she commanded, bounding up the stairs to her tower.

Isaak could do little more than obey, sending a flurry of panic through the kitchen maids, before one of the cooks assured him the Queen would have what she wanted.

Isaak exchanged a rueful grin with the cook. They both knew if the Queen did not get what she wanted, she was not above venturing into the kitchen herself in pursuit of it.

He counted to a hundred, then did it again, before he ascended the stairs to the Queen's bower. She'd changed from a wet gown to a dry one, though it could have been the same one, for it looked exactly the same. The Queen owned grand gowns, but she rarely wore them.

She thumped a small chest on the table, wiping the dust away with her sleeve. "Your uncle left this for you, when he entrusted you to our care."

"My uncle?" This was part of the story he had not heard.

"When your father disappeared, your mother's brother, a knight named Sir Chase, came to court, carrying you and a small sack of belongings. I put them in here for safekeeping, and here they have stayed until now." She beckoned him forward. "Open it."

Isaak reached out and flipped open the lid. Most of the space inside was taken up by a bundled sack. When he upended it on the table, a curious collection of things fell out.

A pair of black boots, so dark they seemed to drink the light from the gold coin sparkling beside them. And a pair of golden brown, fur lined gloves. The boots and the gloves looked worn, like they had been well used.

"They all belonged to your father, or so Sir Chase said. I remember the gloves, and the boots. He would tap his toe three times, and then a hole would open up in the wall or the floor or wherever he wanted it to, and he could walk right through. Wherever the king imprisoned me, he could not keep Abraham out."

"You knew him? You knew my father?" Isaak burst out.

The Queen smiled sadly. "If it were not for your father, I would have died at the mad king's hands. He didn't save me out of kindness, though. He believed I held the key to breaking his family curse. He wanted me to save you. It was all he could talk about, no matter how many times I told him I knew nothing of curses or breaking them. It wasn't until the end neared that we both realised the prophecy he'd been given was not about me at all, but about the child I was carrying. The lost princess."

"The princess who disappeared on the same day as the old king," Isaak said, nodding.

If anything, her smile turned pitying. "That

is the story we told the kingdom, when we asked them to look for her. Even offered a reward, though it has never been claimed. No, and this is something I have never told a soul, and nor must you. The king – King Lubos, my good husband – gave the girl to a witch to protect her from your father. Where the witch took her, I know not…but I know in my very bones that if anyone can cure you and your family of this curse, it is my lost daughter. Which is why I must ask you to find her."

The Queen laid a silver amulet on the table, topped with a milky white stone. "This is a magic amulet, enchanted to help you find your heart's desire. It warms in your hand when you are on the right path, and cools when you are not. I bought it many years ago, intending to use it to find her myself, but…there is always so much work to do, no matter how many apprentices I have, that I fear I may never get the chance to leave the city, let alone try to search for her. Which is why I must send you. If you bring me back my daughter, she will cure you of your curse, and I will grant you your father's castle and lands. You will be a baron in your own right."

Isaak's hand itched to grab the amulet, but he resisted. "What do the gloves do? And the coin?" he asked instead.

The Queen stared at them. "Sir Chase said the gloves are enchanted to resist the curse. When Abraham wore them, he could touch things without turning them into gold. When he took them off, touching things with his bare hands, then everything he touched turned gold."

"And the coin?"

She just shook her head. "I do not know. Only that it belonged to your father, and your uncle wanted you to have it. Perhaps if it has magical properties, they will reveal themselves to you, for neither I nor any witch I have met could find anything enchanted about it."

Isaak packed the boots, the gloves, the amulet and the coin into the sack, then threw it over his shoulder. "When do I leave?" he asked.

"As soon as Romein departs for his mill in the lowlands," the Queen said. "You will leave the city together, and part ways when the amulet draws you in a different direction. You may take any supplies you need from the armoury or the kitchens, and one of my palfreys from the stables. Heaven knows I have little need of them. Just bring my lost daughter home to me, Isaak. That is all I ask."

Isaak bowed. "As Your Majesty commands."

Three

"He must die a slow, painful death. Promise me, Rapunzel. As much pain as possible, for as long as possible," Kun rasped, clutching Rapunzel's shoulder. "Promise me!"

Rapunzel wanted to tell her to save her breath, but she knew Kun would not let this slight against her stand. Even with her dying breath. "Yes, Mother. A prolonged, painful death. I promise."

Only then did Kun subside.

Rapunzel waited until her chest did not rise again, then pushed a pillow beneath her godmother's head. There was little she could do for her now, except begin fulfilling her promise.

So she headed upstairs to her workroom, where her loom waited.

As she ascended the stairs, she let her mind sift through the possibilities. For as long as she could remember, she'd been able to access not only her own memories, but those of all the witches and enchantresses who'd come before her. Hundreds of women who had witnessed countless atrocities, cast all manner of spells, for both good and ill, whose combined experience would surely contain the perfect fate for treacherous King Thorn.

By the time she reached the top of the tower, she was torn between disembowelment and being burned alive.

Yet when she reached her workroom, she remembered that for all his faults, King Thorn was still the king of Aros, and he had no children of his own. His only heir was Prince Vardan and Princess Zuleika's newborn son, who was far too young to rule in his uncle Thorn's place. A regent would be required – one who could rule the prosperous kingdom of Aros for the next twenty years. Whereas Thorn, for all his personal faults, did have one redeeming feature – he was a capable ruler, who took pride in his country's prosperity.

So if Thorn was to die a slow and painful death, for the good of his kingdom, his pain must be prolonged for a good twenty years.

Not disembowelment, then. But if he somehow survived the burning…

Rheumatismus, her memories whispered. A word she did not know, but her memories most certainly did. It was a condition that did not kill a man, but made his joints swell, causing him a great deal of pain. Pain that would slowly incapacitate him over time, and would also twist his hands so that he could no longer hold a sword to stab anyone in the back.

It was a fitting future for King Thorn, who had caused so much pain in his life.

Rapunzel set her loom against the wall, then began to unbraid her hair. Once the dark locks reached the floor, she reached for the shears, and snipped off a thick strand. Then she began attaching the hairs to her loom as warp threads.

When she was done, she opened her basket of silks, in every colour of the rainbow and more besides. Rapunzel might not live in a royal castle, but Kun did not stint her for materials when it came to her weaving. Kun knew the magic Rapunzel's loom could create.

Finally, Rapunzel went to the chest that held the most important materials of all – locks of hair from the powerful men and occasional women Kun had made bargains with. Including the lock of hair she'd obtained from King Thorn, when she'd promised him an heir. Hair that had never needed to be used, for Zuleika was already pregnant with Thorn's nephew.

But now…she had a king's fate to weave. A fate he definitely deserved.

Four

Isaak found Romein in the training yard. "Good morrow, cousin. How goes your suit with Rosaline?" When he'd told Romein about the Queen's quest yesterday, Romein had confessed his own plan to win Rosaline's hand and take her as his new bride when he returned to his father's lands. Isaak had tried to reason with him, but Romein would hear none of it.

Romein growled, attacking the poor apprentice he was sparring against with an unusual show of force.

Instinct drove Isaak between them, pushing Romein's blade away with his own.

"I asked you how you fared with Rosaline," Isaak repeated, though he suspected he already knew the answer. Princess Rosaline had inherited all of her mother's cleverness, but she had also been raised a princess. She would never settle for anything less than a king.

"Out of her favour, where I am in love," Romein said, lunging at Isaak.

Isaak danced back, sword at the ready, as he broke into a grin. "Alas, that love, which I had thought so gentle, should be so tyrannous and rough in proof!"

"He would not be so rough with Princess Rosaline!" the battered apprentice said, wincing as he clambered to his feet.

He would never get the chance, Isaak knew.

"But Princess Rosaline will not have him, for she has her heart set on a political marriage, where she will be a queen like her mother. One such as she will never marry some country lord, whose first love is waterwheels, with which he means to save his country!" Isaak's grin never wavered. "You should forget her, cousin, and go home as you planned. You have learned much from the Queen and from Master Zimmerman. You must now take your knowledge home, and use it to save your people from the floods, as the Queen intended. Meanwhile, Rosaline will likely be married off to some old man who needs heirs, and when she is done labouring for him, she will hear tidings of your triumph, and regret the poor choice she made today. Because you, the hero of your people, will have your choice of ladies falling at your feet."

Romein dropped his guard, holding his free hand up in surrender. "I might save my people from the floods, but if you think I can love another as deeply as I have loved Rosaline, you are mistaken. She is one woman my heart can never forget."

Isaak sheathed his sword. "Ah, but we are both about to set out on impossible quests.

You mean to save your people, a far harder task than winning one woman's heart, if it belonged to anyone but flint-hearted Rosaline, and I am supposed to find and save the Queen's eldest daughter, before my family's curse claims me, as it has all my predecessors. Yet you do not waver. I believe you truly will save your people, and I...the Queen is certain that I will save her daughter, though we both know I am no match for the formidable witch who stole her as a baby." He shook his head. "You speak of impossible quests, and yet..." He longed to tell Romein the truth, the secrets the Queen had entrusted to him, but he could not.

Romein sighed, as if he already knew the heavy burden his cousin carried. "Forgive me, cousin. You are right, of course. The Queen has given me a task that may take a lifetime, but at least I know I shall have that. If you carry your father's curse, you will die young, like all the Rumpelstiltskin men. I pray that you may have your miracle, and that you shall find this girl, who your father believed could break the curse, so that you may live a long and happy life at your family estates, which the Queen will return to you after you find her lost princess. Perhaps one day I shall look forward to a visit from you, so that you can show your new bride my miraculous waterwheels, for surely the princess cannot help but fall in love with the man who saves her from the witch…"

Isaak had to smile at Romein's naivete. Neither of them would marry Molina's daughters. But he would humour him. "If that is so, then we will both have our miracles. I will introduce my bride to yours, as you show me the lands you have saved. Do we have an accord?"

Romein shook Isaak's hand. "Farewell, and may God go with you. For without Rosaline, I travel alone," Romein said.

"But not, I think, for long," Isaak said. Romein would find someone else in his father's lands, and forget all about Rosaline. Isaak gave just as little thought to the lost princess, who he did not believe he could find. He knew what his heart's desire was, and once he stepped through the city gates, the amulet would lead him there, as surely as the sun rose in the east.

Five

Finally, it was finished. Rapunzel tied off the ends and surveyed her work. A painter might have made a better likeness of Thorn, but she recognised him clearly enough. Particularly as the supine figure's hair was formed out of strands of the king's own hair. He lay on his bed with a pained expression on his face, his twisted hands held out before him in supplication to a woman who might have been Kun, but she turned her face away.

"Is it done?"

Rapunzel rose in surprise. "Mother! You should not be up yet. You are still weak from the loss of blood. I was just about to bring this to you. See? A slow and painful death, just like you wanted."

Kun made a rumbling sound in her throat that Rapunzel couldn't be sure if it meant she approved, or not. "There is work to be done. That fool has likely spread the story of my death, so I must counter it, by a show of strength, to show other rulers how false he is. Persuade them to conquer his lands so that they are under the hand of a more capable king…"

"But Mother…" Vardan and Zuleika's son would be a capable king. He would learn to rule from the Master of Beacon Isle, a man who loved his people so much he'd been willing to do anything to save them from the curse.

"Enough, Rapunzel. You have done well." Before the praise could go to Rapunzel's head,

Kun frowned. "But you should not have spoken to Thorn. You should have remained hidden. For if anyone were to find out about your abilities…I could not keep you safe. You are a treasure beyond price. You must remember that."

"Yes, Mother," Rapunzel said, though she had to force out the smile that went with it. She'd heard her godmother say this many times, but it still grated. Just once, she'd like to weave her own future, instead of ensorcelling someone else's.

Worse, the more futures she wove, the more they seemed to resent Kun for the power she had over them. Thorn had not been the first king who'd turned on her, though most had been more polite and less violent.

Kun pressed a hand to her chest and winced. The wound had not healed completely yet, if it still pained her. Not for the first time, Rapunzel wished she had healing gifts instead of her peculiar talent for influencing the future.

Then she had an idea. "If you would give

me a lock of your hair, I could weave a tapestry where you are well again, without pain," Rapunzel said eagerly.

"No!"

Rapunzel recoiled at her godmother's sudden shout.

Kun managed a smile. "No, child, keep your powers for more important things. I will heal from this, as I always do. Miraculous healing, even on the threshold of death, is my gift, after all."

Rapunzel had often questioned this, but never aloud. She'd seen Kun heal from grievous wounds many times, so she knew her godmother did heal most miraculously, but she also knew that the one thing about magic was that the spells one cast rarely affected the caster. So a witch could render herself invisible by making other people's eyes unable to see her, but she could not turn herself into a bear, even if she could transform an entire town into animals. And Rapunzel could weave anyone else's future but her own, for hers never changed.

Every morning she woke in the tower, and every night she retired to her bed in the same tower, never to leave.

Just once…she wanted to weave her own fate. If not on her loom, then some other way.

"I don't know why I don't just summon a dragon to burn all their castles to ash, and set new rulers in their places who will listen to me, instead of keeping their own foolish counsel," Kun grumbled.

Rapunzel prayed she would not be called upon to make that future a reality. Burning King Thorn alive was one thing, but other innocent people? No. She wanted a future without this tower, and definitely free of dragons.

"At least I have you to help me. Such a good girl. If I had known when your parents gave you to me to protect how helpful you would be, perhaps I would not have been so harsh with them. They did wish to protect you, after all."

"Yes, Mother," Rapunzel said. She was not so forgiving. What parents willingly gave up their child? If she were ever lucky enough to have a child, she would not treat them so.

But to have a child, she would need a lover, a virile man the likes of which she never saw in this tower. Only ever from a distance, or through a portal when Kun came home.

If only her parents would come to claim her, now she was of age to marry. Surely they had a prince in mind for her. She was a princess, after all.

Six

When Isaak was out of sight of the city walls, with only forest on either side of the road, he held the amulet in his hands and closed his eyes. Yes, he would like to find the lost princess, if only to please the Queen who'd been like a mother to him all his life. But it wasn't his mother who was in his thoughts now.

No, it was Abraham von Rumpelstiltskin. Baron and traitor and father.

If Isaak could find him, then he could ask his father what had truly happened between him and the old king. Whether his father really was a traitor. If he was, then Isaak would be honour bound to bring him to the King for justice. But if he wasn't, then Isaak would do everything he could to clear his father's name.

He slid down from his horse and stood in the middle of the road, then turned slowly on the spot, the amulet clasped between his hands. When it warmed, just as the Queen said it would, he dared to open his eyes. He was facing a narrow game trail that led off the road and into the woods.

All this time, had his father been hiding in the woods outside the city, waiting for Isaak to find him?

Isaak scrambled back onto his horse and headed into the trees.

Seven

When Kun was well enough to depart the tower again, muttering something about only doing business with sensible kings as the portal closed behind her, Rapunzel breathed a sigh of relief.

Finally, she could see the outside world again.

She crept into Kun's bedchamber and faced the mirror that hung on the wall. It looked for all the world like any normal mirror, if a little larger than most, which might hang in any noblewoman's bedchamber.

But Rapunzel knew better. She breathed on the glass until it fogged, then bit her lip hard enough to taste blood. "Show me my parents," she whispered.

The fog cleared, and she could see into a tower room, not unlike this one. Except the tapestries on her mother's wall were not silk windows into the future.

"I still don't think it is a good idea. You've heard the stories, the same as I have. Thorn likes his women quiet and obedient, and he does terrible things to anyone who offends him. Rosaline would never suit him. Now, if someone were to find little Tessarina, she might be a suitable match. Being brought up by a witch, she is surely far humbler than Rosaline. She would suit him perfectly."

"Enough about her. She is lost, and it is time you accepted she will never return. The witch took her, and if she meant to return her, she would have done so already. Face it,

Molina, the girl is likely dead. But Rosaline is alive, and the only daughter we have who might cement this alliance to Aros with a marriage. She does not object to the union, so I do not understand why you do. He is a king, and you are a queen. Rumours and gossip are beneath you both. No matter what rumours you might have heard, that is all they are. Thorn would treat Rosaline with all the honour and respect a queen of equal rank to his own deserves."

"But if you would only wait until Isaak returns. If he finds Tessarina…" Molina began eagerly.

Lubos sighed. "I can wait a month. Two, at most, while Rosaline prepares her bridal trousseau. But King Thorn will marry our daughter, whether you object or no. Father might have considered all our neighbours enemies, but I am determined to turn every one of them into allies again, if it takes me all my life. Your devices make delightful gifts once the friendship is struck, but if you want more apprentices, and more widespread use of your waterwheels, we must first make friends, before stealing their children and building strange structures in their bailey."

Rapunzel waved the mirror into blankness again, then sat down heavily on Kun's bed. Her godmother Kun was all the mother she'd ever known, for all she knew Molina had given birth to her. Lubos, the father she'd never actually met, had given her to Kun to prevent Molina from handing her over to some baron who'd promised Molina the crown she now wore.

No wonder they were Lubos and Molina to her, not Father and Mother. She was just a thing to them, something that could be traded for position or favour. Ah, but she had a name, at least. Tessarina. A mouthful, but then so was Rapunzel. Or Rosaline, the sister who was doomed to marry King Thorn, for even if her parents did send someone to fetch her from the tower, Rapunzel would never agree to bed that bastard. Then again, if the rheumatismus took hold, perhaps he would not be fit to bed anyone, ever again.

Oh, but there'd been another name they'd mentioned. What was it? Isaak. A name she could not put a face to, and she'd spent hours before this mirror, learning about all the ruling royals throughout the world. Or at least the ones Kun had mentioned.

She breathed on the mirror again. "Show me Isaak."

A boy…nay, a man, though a young one, appeared in the mirror, wearing golden armour as he sat atop a fine horse. Both were dusty and travel worn, as though they'd been riding for some time.

And yet…she could not stop staring at this golden boy, for his hair and gloves were the same colour as his armour, and something about him seemed to draw her gaze, as if a nimbus of magic surrounded him, calling to her.

"Show me everything about him." The words left her lips before she'd even thought to ask them, but the mirror obeyed.

Dressed in court clothes, in her parents' court, every head turned to stare as he passed. Oh, he was easily the most striking man she'd ever seen, and everyone else seemed to think so, too. Even her younger sister, Rosaline, looked at him with longing, though he never dared to raise his eyes so high.

Yet behind him came the whispers, about his past, his family, and his future.

Cursed.

Son of a traitor.

A hostage to his family's good behaviour, taken on the night the old king died.

The Queen's ward.

No lands of his own.

Doomed to die young…

The more she watched, the more she heard, the harder it was to tear her eyes away.

Isaak. The traitor's son, coming to find her to redeem his family's reputation.

He was coming for her. And she could scarcely wait for him to arrive.

Eight

Isaak followed the game trail for what felt like hours, but was likely much less, until he found the cottage. Summer grass had taken root in the thatch, so it looked more like a small hillock in the middle of the clearing than a cottage at first, until he saw the stone wall beneath.

He stopped. This could either be a very bad idea, or a good one.

He prayed that luck would be with him.

After all, the amulet had guided him here, and the Queen wouldn't have given him a faulty amulet.

So Isaak took a deep breath, cupped his hands to his mouth, and shouted, "Ho, the cottage! I'm a traveller. I wandered into the woods and haven't been able to find my way out again. Might I trouble you for a drink and some directions?"

But nothing stirred.

Isaak dismounted and led his horse around to the front of the cottage, where he might knock on the door.

He'd heard enough stories in his childhood about witches living in isolated cottages in the woods to know that anyone who barged into such a witch's house uninvited would be lucky if he lived long enough to regret such rudeness.

But the amulet had led him here, which meant the cottage must belong to his father, not some witch.

Isaak tapped at the door. "Hello? Does

anyone live here?" He knocked again, louder this time.

Still no response.

Finally, he pushed the door open. "Hello?"

Sunlight streaming through the collapsed roof blinded him, and Isaak coughed as the door kicked up a cloud of dust from a flagstone floor that could not have seen a broom in a decade at least. Maybe longer.

No one lived here, except maybe rats.

Isaak kicked aside a bundle of thatch, and found a chair beneath it. Crudely carved, it had fared better than the table that had been crushed when the roof collapsed atop it.

Then the glitter of gold caught his eye, amid the mouldy straw. Isaak swept his booted foot through the mess, which only made whatever it was shine brighter. He reached down and pulled out a gold coin, which could have been the twin to the one the Queen had given him. The one she'd said had belonged to his father.

He pulled it out to compare the two, and if not for the dust, they might have been struck from the same die, only a moment apart. The same strange symbol in the middle, surrounded by a ring of random letters that meant nothing to him.

Isaak seized the amulet. "I said I wanted to find my father!" The amulet burned hot in his hand, until he was forced to drop it. It sat on the floor in a pile of mouldering thatch, smoking slightly as if it, too, was fuming.

The amulet believed his father was here, yet it was patently obvious that no one lived here, and no one had for a very long time.

Isaak sighed and pocketed the coins. Then he proceeded to search the cottage for any signs of life. Twice, actually. On the second pass, the rats he'd unearthed in the corner beneath the remains of the bed had departed to safer places.

No matter what the amulet told him, his father wasn't here. Had not lived here for years, if he ever had. For why would a baron with his own castle and lands take up residence in a tiny cottage on the outskirts of the capital?

Yet none of what he'd heard of his father made any sense.

Then again, Isaak had just spent most of his day rummaging through the ruins of a cottage. If Romein saw him, he'd laugh himself sick, and swear he'd gone mad. Isaak wasn't sure he'd be wrong, either.

So, with a strange ache forming in his chest, he laid out his bedroll beneath the part of the roof that hadn't fallen in, and decided to sleep on it. Things would look clearer in the morning. He was certain of it.

Nine

Rapunzel could not sleep. Her thoughts darted to Thorn, with that beastly look on his face as he held the sword dripping with Kun's blood, before returning to Isaak. The golden boy her mother had sent for her. To save her, only to give her to that beast.

But if she could choose her own fate…

She would choose neither. Not this tower, endlessly weaving futures for the kings Kun favoured, or in Thorn's castle, where she would be forced to obey his every wish. And if he discovered the future she had woven for him…Rapunzel shuddered. No, she didn't dare meet the man. What if he recognised her? A beast who would run Kun through with his sword for actually giving him what she'd promised…what would he do to Rapunzel?

Better to throw herself upon the golden boy's mercy. A man with no lands and no title, only a ruined family reputation, with nothing to lose…

A man who charmed women as easily as breathing. Rosaline might not have deigned to grant him her favour, but plenty of other court women had not been so chaste.

What would it feel like, to have that long, powerful golden body pumping between her thighs? The mirror had shown her his lovers' blissful faces, though Rapunzel's gaze had always been drawn back to him.

Whatever her future held, it must hold him, she promised herself. She might not be able to weave it on her loom, but she would find a way. All her life, she had been good and obedient. But now…she meant to take her life for her own.

Rapunzel began to construct a plan.

Ten

Isaak started awake, aware something was horribly wrong, but unable to work out what.

The pain in his chest had increased during the night, but that wasn't what had woken him.

Light filtered faintly into the room, which he recognised was definitely not his chamber in the castle. He reached out, touching straw, and then something cold and hard. Cursing, Isaak struggled to his feet, so that he might see his surroundings properly.

As sleep left him, memories from yesterday began to assail him. Searching for his father and finding the fallen down cottage. Searching but not finding him. If the amulet had led him here, he would have to admit the truth he did not want to face — that his father had died young, as those with the curse were supposed to, and his body lay here beneath the earth. The amulet had led him to his father's grave, for what other explanation could there be?

He lay down again on his bedroll, looking up at the hole in the roof. What he'd thought was moonlight was actually the brightening dawn. Light glittering so brightly he had to shield his eyes.

What in heaven's name…?

The truth dawned on him like an executioner's axe.

The pile of straw thatch that had fallen from the roof had turned to gold.

With trembling hands, Isaak reached for a patch of mouldy straw. The moment he touched it, it, too, turned to gold.

He swore.

Instead of him finding his father, his father's curse had found him. Now his days were numbered, and no amount of gold could compensate him for that.

Eleven

Isaak took the sack in his teeth and tossed the contents on the floor. Only when he pulled on the gloves did he dare touch anything. With the gloves on, he could pick up the sack and put the boots back in, without them turning to gold. Breaking his fast and saddling his horse took far longer than it should have, and he decided to fill one of his saddle bags with some of the straw he'd turned to gold. After all, it might be useful.

Finally, he pulled out the amulet and held it in his gloved hands. What his heart desired most now was a cure for the curse. If the Queen was right, as she usually was, this would show him the way. He slowly turned on the spot, until the amulet grew hot enough for him to sense the heat through his gloves. He opened his eyes to the rising sun.

East he would go, then.

East and east and further east, as the forest gave way to hills and then mountains, and still the amulet told him to head east. Where he could, he bought provisions, but occasionally he'd had to string his bow and hunt. All that target shooting in the castle bailey had not been time wasted, for he could bring down prey with surprising ease. Cooking the creatures...well, that took more practice. Luckily, he did not mind his meat burned.

The further he travelled, the less familiar everything became. First the plants and animals, followed by the people, and even the words they spoke. Eventually, his only means of communicating was to mime eating, drinking or sleeping, then hold out some of his gold, in the hope they would understand what he sought to buy.

At least the curse had one benefit – he never ran out of gold to pay for what he needed.

Until finally, his path led him to a closed gate, set in a mighty wall that blocked the road ahead. He tried the gate, but it did not budge.

He set up camp for the night, but when the sun rose, the gates were still closed, so Isaak packed up camp and prepared to walk along the walls in the hope of finding another way in.

Until he found the boots that had belonged to his father.

What had the Queen said? Tap three times to open a portal?

Well, it wasn't like there was anyone here to laugh at him if he failed…

Isaak swapped the black boots for his own, and tapped the wall three times. To his surprise, a hole appeared in the wall, wide enough for him to lead his horse through. He didn't hesitate – through they went.

On the other side of the wall stood a garden that stretched for as far as Isaak could see — trees and bushes filled with flowers or fruit, like an orchard large enough to feed a whole city. Yet there wasn't another soul in sight.

But there was a path, little more than a game trail, that led upward.

And when Isaak stepped onto that path, the amulet grew hot. So he ignored the fruit laden boughs on either side of him, and walked on.

For most of the morning, he ascended the slope, marvelling at the size of the garden, which showed no signs of ending. It must have taken an army of men to keep it in such tidy order, yet he didn't see a single person.

Finally, the orchard ended, as the ground grew stony. And from this barren ground rose a tower…a tower with no entrance, though he walked all the way around it.

Well, if there was no other way in…

Isaak tapped the wall three times, waited for a portal to open, and stepped through.

Twelve

Rapunzel knew the moment the stranger entered her tower. It could not be Kun, for she had not seen the blinding light that accompanied one of her godmother's portals. Yet she knew she was not alone.

She set down her sewing and headed down the stairs. Her bedchamber and Kun's were empty, which left only the dining hall and the larder beneath it. The dining chamber looked exactly as she'd left it after breaking her fast, so the stranger was not there.

Down to the larder, then.

Only one small horn window let in the afternoon light, but it was enough.

"It's you," she said in wonderment, staring.

Night after night, she'd dreamed of him, and she'd wept upon waking when she realised it was only a dream. But now…now…

His lips were warm as they moulded to hers, his shoulders hard and strong beneath her hands. The golden breastplate clanked to the floor, but he only kicked it away as he struggled to take his tunic off after it.

Her fingers tangled in the lacing of her dress, but she didn't dare look down to see, for if she did, he might stop kissing her or vanish altogether, and this would be another dream. Finally, the strings binding her eased, and she could slip her dress down over her shoulders to let it pool at her feet, followed by the shift she did not need.

Meanwhile, he'd toed off his boots and his hose remained for only a moment before they, too, were gone.

"Take me, Isaak, claim me for your own!" she begged as she embraced him – the golden boy she had dream of for so long. "Please!"

The stone wall was cold at her back, but the heat of him pushing inside her drove all thought of anything else out of her head. She was ready to explode with pleasure at his first thrust, yet she did not, as the blissful waves within her only grew more and more powerful until she could not help but be swept away, crying out his name as she clung to him.

Better than watching him in the mirror. Better than dreams. Better than anything she could have ever imagined.

He took her up against the wall, until her knees gave out, and then on the floor, her head pillowed on a sack of rice as she moaned incoherently at the sensations he aroused in her body. Deep inside, where no one else had ever touched. The places that belonged to him alone.

Finally, when she thought she could take no more, he drove deep inside her to the hilt, filling her completely, and something seemed to explode inside her, as bright light blinded her.

It took her a moment to realise the lights were not her imagination, but coming from upstairs, higher up in the tower.

Kun had returned!

She let out a soft sob as she pushed him away, hating the feel of his body leaving hers. "You must go! Quickly, for if she discovers you are here. Go, go!"

"The witch who kidnapped you? She is here? I will fight her, and I shall save you!" Isaak declared, pulling on his tunic.

Rapunzel laughed. Foolish, foolish man. "You are no match for her. She is too powerful, for you or even me. You must go. I will…send you a signal when it is safe to return. I will hang a cloth from the highest window in the tower." She leaned in for another kiss, for she could not help herself.

"I will return," he promised. Then a hole opened up in the wall, he stepped through, and he was gone.

Thirteen

Standing outside the tower in his tunic and boots, clutching the rest of his things to his chest, Isaak's mind couldn't seem to grasp what had just happened. Oh, he'd just made love to a very eager girl in a store room, for he could still feel her body wrapped around his, though she was now on the wrong side of the stone wall that separated them, but…but…

She'd known his name. How had she known his name?

Could she actually be the lost princess?

If she was, then he'd been even more of a fool. He should have said something, asked her name, before he'd…well, she'd…and then they'd…and he'd…oh God, Queen Molina would execute him for sure. Or King Lubos would. Because deflowering a princess was definitely treason. As if his father hadn't blackened their name enough, he'd now gone and ruined whatever honour he might have hoped to reclaim.

But he couldn't leave. The amulet had led him here, and he'd promised the Queen to bring the princess home. So when she…what was it? Hung a flag in the window? When she did that, then he could return, and ask her all the questions he should have done instead of getting naked and…

God, that had felt good. He'd bedded girls before, but it was like she'd been made for him. And he'd been made for her, for he'd felt her clench around him more than once, as she cried out his name.

How had she known his name?

Yet another question he would ask her when he saw her again. Because he would see her again. If only to thank her for the amazing lovemaking.

But now, he needed to move away from the tower, if there was a powerful witch in it, if only to assess the situation and work out how to defeat her, so that he might rescue the princess. If indeed she was the princess.

He found his horse had wandered deeper into the garden, and was now grazing happily beneath a peach tree that stood apart from the rest. From here, he had a good view of the top of the tower, and the shuttered windows. No cloth flag flew to invite him in yet, so he set up camp beneath the tree's heavily laden boughs. At least he would not want for food while he waited for the witch to leave.

Fourteen

"All men are fools! The moment they see a pretty girl, they think of nothing but the gristle dangling between their legs. No brains or sense at all!" Kun complained as she brushed imaginary dust from her boots.

Rapunzel could feel a blush heating her cheeks. She was no better, for all she could think of was Isaak's manhood between her legs, and how much she wanted him again. How they would still be in the larder, making love into the night, if Kun had not returned.

But Kun was too busy raging at the foolishness of men to notice Rapunzel's distraction. "Now, take King Xylander of Castrum. Your blood uncle, no less. A little too fond of hunting and jousting in his youth, but a far more fitting monarch for Castrum than that flighty queen of his. Makes you wonder how a wise ruler like Artorius could sire a girl as silly as Zurine. She's given him a whole company of heirs. Enough to outnumber Artorius's old company of knights, though Lancelot is still around, serving the dowager queen. Yet all Xylander can think about is bedding that wife of his. I told him a plague is coming, one worse than anything we've seen before, and it will kill them all unless those with the power to protect the people actually do what they are supposed to, and he waves me away and says he must attend to his wife. He does not care that his people will die if it means he will miss a few more minutes between his wife's thighs!"

Rapunzel had seen King Xylander…and his sister, the Dowager Queen Guinevere, in the mirror. Her uncle and aunt, who had fled the mad king before her father had claimed his throne. It had all happened long ago, before she was born, but she'd often lingered to watch Guinevere fly her falcons over the lake beside the hunting lodge where she lived. Falcons and hawks and occasionally even a mighty eagle flew from her wrist, and she talked to all of them like they were her children. Rapunzel had envied the birds their freedom, but she'd also wished for an animal companion to lessen her loneliness when Kun went away. Until she'd seen the mess the birds made in the mews one day when Guinevere had gone in there while Rapunzel was watching. Guinevere had servants to clean up after her, but Rapunzel had none.

Then the rest of Kun's words sank in. "There's a plague coming that will kill us?"

Kun waved away Rapunzel's concerns. "Oh, not us, of course. We'll be safe here in the tower. But in the towns and cities it will spread like wildfire just like it did before, and no mountains will stop it. The only sensible leader to be found then was Zoticus. This time, we must be prepared!"

"But…isn't Master Zoticus an assassin? I thought he killed people, instead of saving them?" Rapunzel ventured.

"He's old and frail now. I don't think he's killed anyone in years. But he did save a whole town once. But even old and frail, he's a force to be reckoned with. I suspect if he truly wanted a man dead, even now, that man would meet with a terrible accident that no one could possibly have foretold."

A chill closed around Rapunzel's heart. Old or not, he sounded like a very dangerous man. She would look for him in the mirror later, to see how he had saved that town. Anything that might help her survive a coming plague…

"I did not wake you, did I? I forget that we are so far east here. It was still daylight in Castrum when I left, yet here it is after dark."

Rapunzel shook her head. No, she'd been busy rutting with Isaak in the larder.

"I should probably go to bed, though," she said. Where she might dream of Isaak, and how much more they might do on his return.

"So should I. If Xylander will not listen to sense, then I must find other rulers who will. Ones who might influence such fools, or if that fails, invade them. For there is not enough magic in the world to protect us all from this plague, and I will not have centuries of work undone by some damned disease. May as well burn everything to ash with dragonfire." Kun kept muttering equally alarming threats, but she waved Rapunzel good night, so the girl headed upstairs to her own bedchamber.

She opened the shutters a crack to peer outside, hoping she might see him, but all she could see was the garden below, stretching out into the darkness. She prayed she would see him again, and that Kun would leave again soon.

Fifteen

Isaak watched and waited, but the shutters stayed closed, with no cloth in sight. Was the witch punishing her? Forcing her to do who knew what sort of hellish things to fuel her dark spells? He'd heard no screams or any other sounds that might alarm him, but the stone walls of the tower were thick, and with all the windows shuttered…would any sound be audible here?

A dozen times a day, he decided to return to

the tower to see if she was all right, and a dozen times a day, he changed his mind and picked a peach from the tree that had sheltered him from sight during the night.

By the third day, he was heartily sick of peaches. Worse, the fruit juices turned his gloves sticky, and he dared not take them off. So he was forced to hike down to the bottom of the garden, where a spring bubbled up from the rocks beside the wall to wash them, and then endure the wet gloves until they dried.

The pain in his chest, which had been his constant companion since the day he'd found the fallen down cottage in the forest, had eased, until he barely felt it at all.

Yet as he looked up at the tower, wishing and hoping to see something in the window that did not appear, he began to feel a different ache – for her.

That way lay madness, he told himself. If she was the lost princess, she was far too high for the likes of him. If the King and Queen never found out what they'd done, perhaps he'd be allowed to keep his head.

If she wasn't the lost princess, then he would have to resume his quest. He could not stay here with her.

But whoever or whatever she was, that didn't stop him from dreaming about her. Of laying her down on his bedroll beneath the peach tree, and making love to her all night. Hearing her breathy moans as her pleasure built, until she screamed his name over and over.

While he…still did not know her name.

His eyes darted to the tower again, as it did countless times a day. Only this time, something fluttered from the window at the top of the tower, where the shutters hung open.

Isaak scrambled to his feet. He had been summoned.

Sixteen

Once again, Rapunzel knew when he entered the tower. But this time, she was prepared. She'd already steamed the rice and the chicken, and the vegetables were almost done when she ventured up into the top of the tower to hang a flag in the window. She'd decided to use an old gown that she'd spilled wine on when Kun was teaching her to brew. She'd washed it several times, but the cloth had drunk the wine so eagerly, it would not come clean. She only wore it now when she had to do particularly dirty jobs, for the gown was already ruined.

And when she came down to check on dinner…he was there.

"Come up to the kitchen. The noon meal is almost ready," Rapunzel called.

Footsteps sounded on the stairs, and there he was. Not wearing the armour today, just a tunic. He still had those golden-brown gloves, though. But he just stood in the doorway, looking terribly awkward.

Then he bowed. "I thank you for your hospitality, mistress. I am Isaak von Rumpelstiltskin, son of Baron Abraham von Rumpelstiltskin, now ward to Queen Molina and King Lubos of Flamand, where I have spent most of my life. It is out of gratitude for the Queen's kindness that I have come, seeking the Queen's lost daughter."

Not lost, Rapunzel thought, but she didn't say it aloud. If she'd promised her child to some stranger, she would not tell people about it either.

"Yes, well, they call me Rapunzel here," she said, spooning the rice into two bowls, before adding the chicken and vegetables. "We're a long way from Flamand, or wherever else you're from. The sun rises and sets much earlier here."

He looked puzzled. He probably wasn't used to travelling by portal, then. Well, it was a rare gift even among those who possessed magic. She couldn't cast them, though she'd tried. In fact, the only living people she knew of who could cast portals were Amani, Zuleika and Kun herself.

"Let's eat," she suggested, sitting down before the nearest bowl. She picked up her chopsticks.

Isaak took his own seat, then stared down into his bowl. "I don't suppose I can trouble you for a spoon?" he asked.

Kun had said they did things differently in the west. Rapunzel had not realised that included eating rice with a spoon, like a baby. But Isaak seemed uncomfortable enough already – she didn't want to make him feel unwelcome.

She dug out a wooden soup spoon and held it out to him.

He took it carefully in his gloved hand. "Thank you."

She couldn't help but wince at how clumsy he was. After he'd dropped the same piece of chicken three times, she blurted out, "It would be much easier if you took off your gloves."

He stared at her for a long moment, as if weighing her soul. Then, he slowly pulled off one glove, finger by finger, before laying it on the table. He reached for the spoon.

Rapunzel swore.

Isaak dropped the now golden spoon on the table. "Please forgive me. It is a curse. I cannot help it. Anything I touch turns to gold. That's why I wear the gloves."

Now she thought about it, he hadn't even taken them off when they'd made love in the store room. She'd been too wrapped up in the moment to notice at the time, but now…

"Even me?"

He ducked his head as he flushed. "I believe so. Only with my hands, though. Not…other parts." If anything, he turned even redder.

Rapunzel nodded. "Well, the spoon's gold now. No turning it back, I suppose. But you can still eat with it, right? The food will still be food?"

He brightened. "Yes. I've heard of kings who ate off golden plates, they were so rich, which I most certainly am not, but I would be happy to offer you a golden spoon, and a golden bowl to match, in thanks for your hospitality."

How would she explain golden spoons and bowls to Kun when she returned? "No, you keep the spoon. We have plenty more ordinary ones where they came from, and they are easier to wash."

"You are kindness itself, Mistress Rapunzel. I am already so deeply in your debt, that it pains me to ask for more, but I must. I am on a quest to save the lost princess. Will you help me?"

Rapunzel carefully set down her chopsticks. "Come, Isaak von Rumpelstiltskin, son and ward of…whatever you said. We both know you did not come here to save some princess. The reason you are really here is so that I can save you. So the real question is…what would you offer me, to persuade me to save you?"

His mouth dropped open. He stared at her for a long moment before he managed to close it again. "Anything," he managed to say. "Everything. Name it, and if it is within my power to grant it to you, it shall be yours. I swear upon my honour and my life."

She'd wished for so many things over the years, most of which were not within this man's power, or at least she didn't think so. No, what she wanted from him was her freedom…and perhaps his love.

But she'd never broken a curse before, and she didn't dare promise she could unless she knew more.

"Tell me about your curse," Rapunzel said.

So he did.

Seventeen

"And that's all I know," Isaak finished up. "Secondhand stories, when what I need is the truth from my father's own lips. And the more I hunt for him, the more I believe he might already be dead, so I shall never know." He slumped in his seat. He'd finished the meal she'd made, and he couldn't remember tasting any of it.

Rapunzel tapped her chin. "Well, there might be a way…come with me." She beckoned him up the stairs, further up the tower, and he could not help but obey.

"Sit there," she said, pointing at the bed.

"Is this your bedchamber?" he asked. If it was, then they should have made love here, instead of on the floor of the store room. He would not make that mistake again. She deserved softness, and comfort, and every courtesy he could offer.

"No. This room belongs to Mistress Kun. The witch," Rapunzel said.

About to sit on the bed, Isaak recoiled in horror. "Does she not permit you to sleep in a bed? Does she keep you in some underground dungeon instead, only letting you leave when she is not here?" Rage boiled through him. "We must leave here at once. Come, I shall take you safely home to your family." He held out his hand.

Rapunzel only shook her head. "I am safer here than anywhere else in the world. And of course I have a bed. My bedchamber is on the level above. I did not bring you here for the bed, but for the mirror." She pointed at the unusually large mirror on the wall. "It's magic. It allows you to see…whatever you wish to see. People, places, events. The past. Sometimes, very rarely, a glimpse into the future. The first time I used it, I believed as you do – that Kun was holding me prisoner, instead of keeping me safe, and that my family could not possibly have given me to her, as she said. Yet in the mirror's depths, I saw the truth in her words for myself. My mother promised me to the man who could turn straw into gold, so that she might stay with the man she loved. And my father…he gave me to Kun, in exchange for saving my mother's life."

Now it was Isaak's turn to shake his head. Not Molina and Lubos. They'd taken him in, and raised him as their own, though he was a traitor's son. They loved their children. All of them. The look in Molina's eyes when she spoke of the lost princess…

"I'll show you. Then you'll see," Rapunzel said, striding over to the mirror. She breathed on the glass, then whispered something, before standing back again, biting her lip.

A picture that was no longer a reflection of this chamber began to appear in the glass.

And, miracle of miracles, he could hear as though the mirror were a window and not a flat plane of glass.

"Come with me now, and I will save you from the king and your thoughtless husband, and when your child is born, I will see she is treated like the princess she is," the man said, extending his hand. To Isaak's shock, he recognised the man's glove – for he wore its twin on his own right hand.

"I will not leave the man I love. Not for the king, or you, or anyone," the girl said, coughing. "Prince Lubos will return. He will help me, and will marry me, just like he promised." She rose shakily to her feet, staggered to her bed, and fell face-first into the straw. After a long moment, she moved so she lay more comfortably. "I must rest. When I wake, I will…work more."

"Swear to me you will give me the child when she is born, and I will spin all the straw in this room into gold," Abraham said, for it must be him. "You will live and stay with your husband, and your sacrifice will save my life and my son's."

The girl coughed again, more weakly this time. "Give up my child to you? A strange man I neither know nor trust? You are a fool. No. You shall not have her."

Abraham folded his arms across his chest. "Then I will not help you."

The standoff did not last long. The girl fell asleep, and Abraham walked over to the spinning wheel, and began to turn straw into gold.

"She refused him," Isaak said slowly.

Rapunzel looked grim. "At first, she did, but several days later…she did not." She whispered to the mirror again, and the scene changed. Instead of darkness, light filtered dimly into the room where his father sat beside the girl who had become Queen Molina.

Yet her face remained in deep shadow as she whispered, "Yes. If you can spin every bit of flax in this place into gold before the king executes me, then the child is yours."

"Did King Lubos know?" Isaak demanded. Surely he could not have agreed to such a thing.

"When he returned, she was terribly ill, and babbling what he thought was nonsense. He sought magical aid to save her life, and by the time she was lucid enough to tell him what she'd done, it was too late – he'd already promised me to the witch, in order to save my mother's life."

Isaak was lost for words for a long moment. "Both of your parents were willing to trade you, like some…thing?" Queen Molina had been ill, near death, when she'd made her terrible promise, but the King…the King…

With her lips set in a firm line, Rapunzel waved at the mirror again.

A garden appeared, much like the one outside the tower, lit by moonlight.

A shadowy form stood before the gates.

Then she lifted her lantern. "Who dares steal from Mistress Kun?"

Lubos swallowed. "I am Crown Prince Lubos, heir to the king, and I have left fair payment for the plants I took. Let me pass, for a woman's life depends on them."

The witch did not budge. "I decide what is a fair price, not you." Her eyes glowed blue in the darkness. "What is it you have taken? Ah, the rapunzel. You lie, Prince. More than one life depends on the plants you hold."

Lubos hung his head. "'Tis true. The woman I love is carrying our child. We were betrothed to be married, but she has fallen ill, and I fear for her life." He paused, then added, "And for the child."

"What is this woman's life worth to you?" the witch demanded.

"She is worth more to me than everything I own, including my own life," Lubos said without hesitation.

"What would you give me, if I let you leave

with your pilfered plants, and my solemn promise to you that both the woman and her child will live long and healthy lives?"

"Anything," he said.

Rapunzel waved her hand across the mirror, until all they could see was the mirror's reflection.

"He's lucky all she asked for was me. Maybe he feared I was lost to him already, or I would be if my mother died. You don't need to see the rest. He begged and pleaded, until finally, he, too, promised to hand me over."

"But he didn't. The witch stole you," Isaak insisted.

Rapunzel looked at him pityingly. "She did no such thing. Must I show you that, as well?" She did not wait for his answer. She merely breathed on the mirror, and whispered to it.

And the witch appeared, looking younger than before.

"Enter, Your Highness," the witch said, standing before a small cottage.

Lubos stepped forward, holding a small

bundle in his arms. "I come to fulfil the bargain we made. You promised that my wife and child will live long and healthy lives."

The witch's eyes glittered. "And they will. Your queen will outlive you, and hold her son's heir in her arms when your son takes the throne."

Lubos blew out a breath. "And the child? Our daughter?"

The witch grinned. "The little weaver. I have waited a long time for this moment." She held out her arms. "Give her to me."

Lubos crossed his arms over his chest. "Not until you swear to me she will be treated like the princess she is, and cared for as well as her mother might."

The witch laughed. "Princesses are raised to be pawns in a much larger game, married off at the convenience of their fathers to cement this or that alliance. Much like your sister Guinevere, married to a man she does not love. Your daughter will be much more than a bedwarmer and broodmare for one of your allies. She will shape the future of many kingdoms, like one of the ancient queens of legend. I will take her to a place so safe, no one will ever find her to steal or harm her. She will outlive her mother, though she will not bring any kings into the world."

"I will have your word."

"Yes, you are a man of words, when there is so much more to the world. Yet you shall have mine. I swear upon my own life that I will do everything in my power to prolong her life and health. No other girl child will be as precious to her mother as your child will be to me."

Lubos looked down at the child, his reluctance writ clear across his face.

"Give her to me!" the witch demanded, her eyes glowing blue.

Though pain twisted his features, Lubos held out the child.

The witch snatched the child from his arms, and in a flash of light, the witch and the baby were gone, leaving Lubos alone in the garden.

Isaak closed his eyes. "I can scarcely believe

it possible, yet I have seen it with my own eyes. But Lubos was not the only one who made a promise. So did Molina, in promising you to my father. His fury when he found out must have been colossal. Perhaps it was madness that made him turn traitor. Perhaps…"

Pity shimmered in Rapunzel's eyes. "I have never thought to ask what happened after that. If you wish, I will make the mirror show you."

The mirror fogged again, before it showed a dark, stone room, with a woman lying in a bed beside a cradle.

Then a shadowy figure approached the cradle, reaching for the child inside…

"She is gone where you cannot reach her," the girl said.

The shadow jerked upright and turned toward the bed. "You promised her to me. She is the only one who can save my son. I spun you a king's ransom in gold, ten times over, so that you would help me. Faithless woman!"

He raised his hand as if to strike her, then seemed to think better of it, and dropped both hands by his sides again.

"I am Sir Abraham von Rumpelstiltskin, and my son Isaak will be the last of my line, because of you. Many years ago, my ancestor was cursed with the Touch, and he passed it down, father to son, until it came to me. I know not what my ancestor's crime was, but I have done nothing to deserve this fate. My son is but a baby – a few weeks older than your own daughter – and he is innocent. He does not deserve to die young, and see everything he touches turn to cold metal. I beg you, Princess, have pity on a father who only wishes to save his son." Abraham fell to his knees.

Tears trickled down the girl's cheeks as she shook her head. "I am sorry, Sir Abraham, but I cannot. My husband has taken her I know not where, and he will defend her with his life. I could never save you or your son, no matter how much I wish I could. I am merely Molina, a miller's daughter from a barony far to the south of here, with no special powers and no title until the prince married me. My only skill is with a spinning wheel. If I could spin a wheel and change your fate, I would, but fate is a weaver and I have no skill in that. I thank you for everything you have done for me. If not for you, both my daughter and I would be dead at the king's hand. I only wish I could return the favour."

"Then we are lost." He rose to his feet.

Just as Rapunzel raised her hand to wipe the image from the mirror, a sneering voice that belonged to neither Abraham nor Molina forced its way into the room, so loud it sounded like he was here in the tower beside them, and not in this scene from Flamand's past.

"What are you doing in my son's bed, slut? And who is this vagabond? Is his chamber your whorehouse now?"

An angry old man wearing a robe woven from gold thread stepped into view.

"The mad king," Isaak breathed. He'd seen the man's golden statue many times, and it looked exactly like him at this moment.

"Get out. Both of you!" the king snapped. "Guards!"

Abraham pulled off his gloves. "Are you the one who wanted straw turned into gold?"

The king looked smug. "I have all the gold I need. We are now the richest kingdom on the continent. But if I need more, my son's wife will provide. Which is why this slut will get out of his bed, for that is where his wife should lie, while he begets an heir on her!"

The mad king stared at Molina, almost incandescent in his rage. Was he so mad he'd not even recognised his own son's bride?

But the king was so focussed on Molina, he never noticed Abraham rising up in fury.

His bare hands, lifting.

"The princess will spin no more for you. Take your gold, and I hope it makes you happy in hell!" Abraham laid his hands on either side of the king's face, and the king began to scream.

And then…the sound stopped. Where the king had stood, now there was only a golden statue. The one Isaak had seen every day in Flamand's throne room. Not a statue, but the king's glittering corpse. By all that was holy…

"You…you killed the king!" Molina breathed, staring at Abraham in terror.

"He deserved to die," Abraham said simply. "My son will be avenged."

Then Abraham stamped on the floor three times. The flagstones opened up, and he was gone.

Isaak could scarcely breathe. His father was a traitor. He'd killed the king with his curse…and he'd done it for HIM.

"I'm sorry, Isaak. I didn't know. Whatever he did, why he did it…none of it is your fault. There was nothing you could have done. Nothing either of us could have done." Then her arms were around him, and her lips were on his, and for a moment, he could think of nothing but the woman in his arms, and how much he wanted her.

But he forced himself to pull away.

"I want nothing more than to lose myself in

you. But I must know. My father turned traitor for me. I must find him, so that I will know why."

Tears shimmered in Rapunzel's eyes. "He's the reason I'm here. Why Kun – the witch – must protect me. I've grown up knowing he was after me, which is why I've never gone looking for him. Because if I could find him…then he'll also be able to find me."

He took her hands in his gloves, wishing he could touch her properly. "I swear to you, I will protect you from anyone. From everyone. Even my own father, and yours, though he is my king. For if we can find him, we can bring him to justice in Flamand for what he did. Then you will be safe."

She swallowed, looking torn. "It's not just your father who is a danger to me. There are…other things…you do not know…" Then she made her decision. "But if I can help you find him, I shall. Then I will have one fewer man to fear."

Rapunzel stepped up to the mirror, and

breathed on it once more. "Show me Abraham von Rumpelstiltskin," she said.

But the mirror only showed the fallen down cottage where the amulet had led Isaak. The chair beneath the thatch, and the coin in the dust that was now in his pocket.

Isaak shook his head. "That can't be right. There's no one there. I've been there. There's nothing but dust and ruin. No sign that anyone has been there for years!"

Rapunzel wet her lips. "Perhaps…perhaps he is dead, and that is where his body is buried."

He'd had the thought himself, more than once, but it made no sense. If he was dead, then there'd be a body or a grave or something, and he'd examined both the house and the surrounding ground thoroughly. If his father's body was buried there, he'd have found something.

Before he could stop her, Rapunzel said, "Mirror, show me Abraham von Rumpelstiltskin's final moments."

The image shifted, showing the same clearing, this time covered in snow, but the cottage looked nothing like Isaak remembered. This cottage looked lived in, and new, with smoke drifting from the chimney like it was someone's home.

Hoofbeats sounded, and a man on horseback rode into the clearing.

Abraham slid down from his horse, then fell to his knees in the snow.

A man Isaak did not recognise opened the door and stepped outside.

"So you are not as much of a fool as I thought," the man said. He took the horse's bridle, leading the animal toward the stable.

Abraham seized his cloak. "I am a fool. Such a fool. The princess is his only hope. Isaak's only hope. When I am gone, you must take the boy to her and tell her. The king is dead. And the princess…the princess…the seer was right about the boy. She cannot be wrong about the princess. She is Isaak's only hope."

The other man shook himself free. "Go inside, and warm yourself before the fire. I will see to the horse, and you should see to your son."

The man walked out of view, and Abraham entered the cottage, rubbing his left shoulder as if it pained him.

Abraham sat on the chair by the fire, holding out his bare hands to the flames to warm them. His fingers were a peculiar shade of grey-blue.

"Oh, Maja," Abraham sighed.

Then he grimaced, clutching at his chest. His face began to pale, then turn as blue as his fingers.

His mouth gaped open, but no sound came out. Then his eyes closed, and he slumped, lifeless, against the back of the chair. A moment later, fog seemed to coalesce around him, hiding him from sight. A faint clinking sound came from the cloud, but it was impossible to see what made the noise.

And then the fog was gone, taking Abraham

with it.

A pair of dark shoes lay on the floor, full of gold coins that spilled out in a puddle on the flagstones. A pile of coins sat on the chair, too, topped by a pair of familiar golden brown, fur lined gloves. Of Abraham, there was no sign.

With shaking hands, Isaak pulled the two gold coins from his pocket.

"Show me Abraham's body," he whispered to the mirror.

But the mirror only showed him his own reflection, and those two gold coins.

"Show me where Abraham lies now," Rapunzel ordered, tapping the mirror.

But the image never changed. If anything, the coins seemed to grow larger, until all he could see was his own hand, and the coins in his palm.

Eighteen

Isaak seemed lost, and Rapunzel's heart could not help but ache for him. At least her father still lived, while his had died without even leaving a body behind so that he might be mourned.

She offered him her hand, and he took it, allowing her to guide him upstairs to her bedchamber, where she pushed him down on the bed, telling him to rest. Only when she started pulling off his boots, he began pulling other things off, too, and then so had she, and then he'd pulled her down onto the bed beside him, and…

Oh God, he felt so good inside her. Hot and hard and so delicious she could not help but moan and beg for more.

She lost count of the number of times she screamed his name, as his gloved hands held fast to her hips, driving ever deeper inside her, grinding against her, until she thought she could bear no more pleasure, and he found his own shuddering release.

She drowsed in his arms as he drifted off into sleep, and, she hoped, dreams that would be far pleasanter than the events she'd shown him in the mirror.

But even as she ached, both for the lovemaking they'd done and her need for more, her thoughts went back to Abraham's final moments. The coins coming out of the fog. There'd been magic at work there, she was certain of it, and if she could understand how it worked, then maybe she could figure out how to break the curse that bound Isaak. So that he might take off his gloves and caress her with his bare hands, and do all manner of pleasurable things that she'd seen him do in the mirror. Joys other girls had known, before the curse had stolen touch from him. And her.

And there it was, wasn't it? She would save him – would move heaven and earth to do it – because whoever had cursed his family had no right to curse her as well. If Kun had taught her one thing in all the years they'd lived together in this tower, it was that those in power were no match for a witch who could shape the future.

Her own parents had traded her away so that they might live with the person they loved. Was it so wrong if she wanted to use her powers to save someone so that she might have love in her life, too? She'd be saving his life, after all.

Having made up her mind, Rapunzel slid out of bed, pulling on some clothes to protect her from the cold, and headed back to Kun's room to ask the mirror for more.

Nineteen

"Show me the original casting of the Rumpelstiltskin curse," Rapunzel whispered, biting her lip until she drew blood.

The mirror misted, then cleared. A cottage in a clearing, not unlike the one where Abraham had died. But the trees were different – older, darker.

Through the trees rode a man in leather armour, upon an enormous black horse. He, too, clutched his chest.

He slid down to the ground. "I seek the witch!" he bellowed. He grimaced with the effort, but still he managed to stand tall as he strode toward the cottage.

The witch emerged, her arms folded across her chest. Rapunzel's breath caught in her throat. It was Kun, she was certain of it. But older, somehow. Could Kun have cast the curse that kept Isaak from touching her? The same one that had killed his father? No, surely not.

There was pity in Kun's dark eyes as she regarded the man, but she stood firm. "I am sorry, Sir Rumpelstiltskin, but there is nothing more I can do for you. You're dying." Kun turned away.

Isaak's ancestor — for surely that was who this Sir Rumpelstiltskin was — refused to admit defeat. "I may be dying, but there is still something you can do for me."

She sighed. "I assure you there is not, but why don't we go inside and discuss it? I can see you need a pain draught. That, at least, I can give you."

Yes, she knew more about herbs and potions than anyone alive. Kun had travelled the world, and collected healing knowledge wherever she went.

The knight followed Kun inside the cottage, then sank onto a bench while Kun darted about the cottage, assembling what she needed to make the draught.

"Mistress, I have heard tales that you are more than a herbwife and healer. More than a usual witch. There are tales that you are what heathens call an enchantress, a woman who works magic. They say that you have power over earth and rocks, and when a child from the village fell down a well, you cracked open the very earth itself to retrieve her, then commanded the rock to return to its previous place, and it obeyed." The knight's shining eyes fixed on her, as if he expected a miracle.

If he'd lost a child down a well, Kun would certainly help him. Kun might not tolerate the childishness of men, but she was fond of children.

Kun glanced at him. "There are all sorts of tales. Why, I have heard people tell stories of unicorns and dragons and immortality to children around the fire at night."

The knight bowed his head. "There is a story about an ancient king who was granted a wish. He wanted to be the richest man in the world, so he wished for everything he touched to turn to gold. It is said that gold comes from the ground, and a wielder of earth magic might be able to do such a thing."

Kun lifted a bucket of water and poured some of it into a small pot over the fire. "Then you must also know the end of the king's tale. He could not eat or drink or touch his family, and he feared his wish would kill him, so he washed his wish away in the river, and shunned gold for the rest of his days."

Rapunzel smothered a laugh. She remembered that story. She would not have done what the king did. No, she would have spent every moment turning everything she could into gold before hunger or thirst overcame her, and only then would she have been willing to wash away the curse. For then she would have all the gold she needed, and a future with her family. Even the worst curse might be twisted in order to bring good fortune, though it might have been created for ill.

Kun had called her silly, and told her it was time to go to sleep. But Rapunzel had thought long into the night about it, planning what she might do if she were cursed. Not that anyone would dare, with a powerful witch like Kun protecting her.

But the knight continued: "I will soon be beyond such mundane things as gold or food or even days, Mistress. But my family will not. And I have spent all that I have in physic for what ails me, seeking a cure that will let me live long enough to restore my family's fortune. If I die now, I will leave them little more than the Rumpelstiltskin house on stilts my father left me, on the rock King Karl granted him for his service. Other knights are building castles along the river to secure their lands, and if my son does not have one, he will lose his lands to a richer man who does. He needs gold, and I would give anything to give it to him."

Kun sat down and squinted at him. "You ask me to curse you. Not for yourself, but for your son, who you will never be able to touch again. You will never be able to eat or drink, and your own wife will not be able to hold your hand as you take your dying breath. You even wish to hasten that dying breath."

The knight pressed his hand to his chest and grimaced. Just as Abraham had done, in those last moments before he died. Was there something amiss with his heart? "Yes. I am no use to them like this. Better to be dead than to be a burden." He took the cup she offered in his grey-blue fingers and drained it.

Kun watched him with pity on her face for a long moment before she said, "There is some truth in the tale, but the enchanter who cast such a spell was a fool. I can restrict the spell to your hands, while you live. You may still eat and drink, as long as your hands do not touch it. But when your heart stops, the spell will spread throughout your body, turning it all to gold."

Was that what had happened to Abraham? The spell had turned his body to gold coins? It would explain why there had been no body to bury, and why the mirror thought the coins Isaak carried around were all that remained of his father.

Kun bowed her head. "This I will do for you, but you must swear to tell no one about the source of your wealth. Breathe a word to anyone that I cast the spell, and that breath shall be your last."

That definitely sounded like Kun. Rapunzel wondered who Kun had enlisted to carry out her vengeance in the time of Isaak's ancestor, for this was long before Rapunzel's birth.

"I swear on my honour, and that of my father, that I shall tell no one," the knight promised.

"Then hold out your hands, palms up," Kun instructed, picking up a knife. She pricked her thumb with the point, then used the welling blood to trace lines on the knight's fingers, then his hands, until she swiped her thumb along the lines on his wrists, right the way around. "By my blood, I bespell yours. Everything your hands touch from this moment until the day you die, will turn to gold."

For a moment, the knight's hands glowed, then lit up in a blinding flash of blue that made him turn his head away.

Rapunzel had to blink away the burning afterglow from her own eyes, for she'd looked away far more slowly than the canny knight.

When the light had faded and it was safe to look again, Rapunzel saw the knight's hands were clean, all the blood gone, though the blue tinge to his fingertips had taken on a greenish hue.

Like he was already dead, though he still drew breath. A terrible curse indeed, but one he had asked for. Rapunzel couldn't suppress a shiver. Isaak's ancestor had been a brave man who cared deeply for his family. How, then could he have allowed the curse to kill his family, generations later? Kun must have cast the spell wrong.

Kun said, "I would offer you a cup of wine to toast your family's fortunes, but..."

The knight grimaced. "No more wine for me, now. It does not agree with the draught you gave me."

Kun nodded. "I have just the thing. One of the dairymaids brought a pail of milk this morning, and it's been chilling in the cellar ever since. I mean to keep the cream for butter, but there will be more tomorrow." She rose and headed for the cellar. When she returned, she carried a brimming jug that she poured into two cups and a bowl.

When she caught the knight eyeing the bowl with curiosity, she shrugged. "That's for Butter. He usually comes running as soon as I go into the cellar, for he loves his milk." She raised her voice, and called, "Butter! Puss-puss-puss!"

Whoever Butter was, he did not come.

With increasing urgency, Kun kept calling, leaving the knight alone in the cottage as she moved outside.

After a while, Kun fell silent. But she didn't come back in.

The knight looked uneasy, as if dreading something.

"You did this!" Kun shrieked, bursting into the cottage. In her arms, she cradled a piece of gold-coloured fur. A dead cat. Tears sprang to Rapunzel's eyes. The poor thing.

The knight's eyes widened in fear as he started out of his seat. He swayed for a moment, before he was forced to sit down again. "I've never seen that cat before," he said weakly.

Kun pointed a shaking hand out the door. "He had a muddy hoofprint on his back that could only have come from that enormous warhorse of yours. You come here for my help, yet you kill my cat without a care? It's not my fault your ailment is beyond my powers. You, Sir Kempenich von Rumpelstiltskin, have no heart, and that is what is killing you. Take your golden curse, but know this: every male born of your blood will bear the same curse. His heart will fail him in his prime, just as yours has, and his only warning will be the curse, heralding his death. And you – " She waved her hand, and Kempenich was lifted off his feet, soaring through the air, before landing in the killer horse's saddle. "You shall have a daily reminder of the creature you killed." Another wave of her hand, and a pair of gloves appeared on Kempenich's hands. Gloves just like the ones Isaak now wore.

But Kun wasn't finished. "As long as you wear these gloves, you may touch things like a normal man. Take them off, and all you touch turns to gold. A curse on you, and all who follow you!"

Now Rapunzel understood. Kun had always tried to help people, while ungrateful louts like this knight thoughtlessly killed her or her cat.

At least Kempenich had the good grace to beg for forgiveness. Thorn had not been so sensible. "Please. Curse me…kill me, do what you will with me, but don't hurt my son," he begged.

Her eyes were the cold of black ice. "Bring my cat back to life, and I will consider it."

"Please…"

Kun clapped her hands. "Go!" The horse galloped off, forcing Kempenich to cling desperately to the reins so that he would not fall off. "And don't return!" she shouted after him.

The mirror followed the knight, swaying so alarmingly in his saddle it was a miracle he didn't fall off, until finally, the creature began to slow. They'd arrived at a wooden house on stilts, built on an island in the middle of a swift river. On the bridge which was the only path to the house stood what appeared to be a blue-green lion.

No, an old, corroded statue of a lion,

Rapunzel realised. So old it was a wonder it was even recognisable. But the knight recognised it, for he smiled at the sight.

Then he pulled off his glove and patted the lion's head. In a moment, the blueish bronze turned into bright, shining gold.

He shoved his hand back into the cat-fur glove, clutching his chest as he cursed witches and their cats.

It was the last thing he would ever do, for his face grew pale, then tinged with blue, as he slid from his horse to the ground, gasping for air.

Then his body stilled, and was enveloped in familiar fog. When the fog cleared, nothing remained of him but a pile of gold coins like some pagan offering at the foot of the golden lion statue.

Rapunzel wept for the knight, and for Kun's cat, and for all the doomed sons who had come after him, all the way down to Isaak. It was Kempenich's heart that had killed him, and Abraham's, too. Isaak would be next, if she did not find a way to stop it.

More than ever, she wanted to break the curse, but she had no idea where to start.

Twenty

When Isaak awoke, he was alone in the bed. Daylight glimmered behind the shutters, so he pulled on a tunic and wandered downstairs in search of Rapunzel.

He found her in the witch's bedchamber, whispering strange things to the mirror.

"What's necromancy?" Isaak asked.

"It's a very rare kind of magic. It raises the dead. As I can't imagine any other way a cat might be brought back to life, I thought I'd ask the mirror if there was anyone alive who was actually skilled at that kind of magic. It turns out there is exactly one necromancer in the world – and she just happens to be the only daughter of the world's most deadly assassin." Rapunzel pointed at the mirror, where a dark-haired girl stood beside an enormous white bear.

"She keeps a giant bear for a pet?"

Rapunzel shook her head. "No, he's actually a prince, but he's under an enchantment, so that he can turn into a bear. The way things appear, they'll be a couple eventually, if they aren't already. But there are issues with the succession and bloodlines and some usurper in the past…it's all very complicated. Kun explained it to me once, but even she's not inclined to interfere in matters that involve the assassin's daughter."

She frowned. "Even then, I'm not sure if necromancy counts as bringing someone back to life. I mean, the reanimated dead move and all, but I'm not sure they're actually alive or if it's some sort of telekinesis, which she is also extremely skilled at, because it's still magic that makes them move…"

Isaak raised his hand. "Was I supposed to understand any of that? Because I was taught engineering and archery and swordfighting where I grew up, not magic. And while I know some big words most people don't, I'm pretty sure none of them were in the things you just said."

Rapunzel coloured. "I'm sorry. It's just…wanted to try and find a way to break your curse, and I thought if maybe I could find a way to bring the witch's cat back to life, she might be willing to undo the original spell, or at least take it off you."

Isaak couldn't help but burst out laughing. "You think the witch who cast the spell is still alive? If she was, she'd be hundreds of years old. No, if you want to raise the dead, you'd probably have to start with the witch herself, and then raise her cat."

But Rapunzel wasn't laughing. "Magic can

do all manner of strange things. Nothing is impossible. I could tell you stories…"

Isaak grinned. "And I would love to hear them. It's a long journey home to Flamand, but if you have enough tales to entertain us every night, it will seem like no time at all."

"But I can't leave here, and go to Flamand with you. Kun would never allow me to leave," Rapunzel protested.

"All the more reason to leave before she returns, so she will never know. Pack some food and your belongings, and we can be on our way before the sun is high in the sky. By the time she returns, we will be long gone, and she will never find us."

Rapunzel stared at him like he was the biggest fool who'd ever capered about the court. "But she's a powerful witch, and you've seen her mirror. She has only to ask the mirror to show me to her, and she will be able to cast a portal so that she may instantly appear wherever we are. And…I may not be able to break your curse without her help. If I were to leave with you, she'd never be willing to help you, and she might not forgive me, either. There are…the world is bigger than either of us, and there are things still to come…she's trying to make the world better, Isaak. To shape it into a place where bad things don't happen, or when they do, they aren't so bad for everyone. I'm helping her. She can't do everything, and sometimes…sometimes the men in power think that having a sword makes them right, and allowed to do whatever they please. I can't just leave. Not knowing…all the things I do."

"But, Rapunzel…"

She waved him into silence. "Please. Let's just go down to breakfast. I'll make you some rice porridge and perhaps you can tell me about life in Flamand's court. I'm sure you have some funny stories, more than the little I have seen through the mirror."

Perhaps if he told her enough stories, he would sway her enough to want to come with him. For, short of kidnapping her, he didn't think there was any other way she'd come with him now.

<h1 style="text-align:center">Twenty-One</h1>

He'd made Rapunzel laugh with tales of Romein, Mercutio and the other apprentices, but just as he thought he might have persuaded her that she'd like Flamand, there was a flash of light from above.

The witch had returned.

"Hurry, she cannot find you here!"

Isaak already knew, and he was halfway down the stairs to the store room before she'd finished speaking. "Another flag when it is safe, if you please." At her nod, he hurried down the rest of the way.

He tapped on the store room wall, and was soon outside, running back to his camp under the peach tree. His palfrey did not seem to have missed him at all, for she did not even look up.

Isaak set about making a fire, and setting a pot of stew to cook. It likely wouldn't be as tasty as Rapunzel's cooking, but it would give him the sustenance he needed until he could see her again. Well, that and the peaches, he thought as he plucked one from the tree and bit into the sweet flesh.

"What are you cooking?"

Isaak must have fallen asleep, for it was dark now, and he could scarcely see the woman who'd spoken. He dived forward to add fuel to the fire, lest it go out before his supper was cooked.

"Is there enough for two?"

As the fire brightened, he squinted at his visitor.

A noblewoman, judging by her fine violet gown. Sensible boots peeped out from beneath the hem with every step, instead of the court slippers he would expect such a woman to wear. But she had no horse, and not even a cape around her shoulders, which she would need soon enough, for the nights were cold here in the mountains.

"That depends. Are you the witch?" he demanded.

She inclined her head, considering. "Well, I am a witch, though not the one who lays claim to this place, if there is one. I come from the west, far to the north of Flamand." She held out her hand. "I am Lady Zuleika, from Beacon Isle."

He'd heard her name before, though he couldn't remember where. He gestured for her to take her place at the fire. "You're a long way from home, Lady Zuleika of Beacon Isle."

She gracefully took a seat beneath the peach tree, with her back to the trunk. Like a queen on a throne. "Not much further than you,

Isaak von Rumpelstiltskin. What brings you to the Kunlun Mountains? The divine fruit?" She waved at the boughs above her head.

Isaak snorted. "You are the second woman this week who knows my name without having to ask. Do you have a magic mirror, too?"

Her eyes widened with surprise. "I did once, but no longer. Hence why I must ask: why are you here?"

Isaak shook his head. "If you can believe it, I am waiting for Queen Molina's lost princess to hang a flag in her window, to let me know when the witch holding her prisoner departs, so that it is safe for me to visit her."

Zuleika's mouth dropped open. "You mean the girl is still alive? What would a witch want with a princess? It's not like she is the heir to Flamand – Lubos and Molina have a small army of sons."

She spoke of them as though she knew them – and was familiar or important enough not to use their titles. Yet she could not be much older than he was.

"Rapunzel thinks the witch keeps her to help her make the world better. The witch plays at politics, and somehow Rapunzel is key to her plans. Or so Rapunzel says. I fear the witch has told her many things which sound good, but might not be true. After all, what change can one witch, even a powerful one, make to all the courts of all the world? She would be constantly travelling, hearing everything, to know where she must go next…" But hadn't Rapunzel said she could cast portals, through which she might travel instantly from one place to another? Combined with the mirror, that allowed her to see any place she wished to…

But Zuleika just nodded, as if this was not news to her. Perhaps she had something even better than a magical mirror. "And what news of your father?"

"My father is dead. He died long ago, in a cottage outside the capital, when I was just a baby. Before Queen Molina and King Lubos were kind enough to accept me into their court as their ward." He'd learned this only yesterday, so the wound still felt raw and new. Tears pricked his eyes, but he blinked them away. He would not weep in front of this strange woman. A woman who… "How could you possibly know I went looking for my father?" He jumped to his feet, reaching for his sword, though it lay several yards away, beside his bedroll.

"Peace, peace, young Isaak. I made the amulet that guided you, and Molina thought you might try to use it to find your father. She hoped you would find her daughter, but she knew the girl could not be safe while your father lived, so she asked me to follow you, so that I might deal with him when you found him. I did not expect him to be dead, and the daughter to be alive." She leaned forward and peered into the stewpot. "It seems your supper will be ready soon. Would you like me to serve?"

Isaak held up his gloved hands. "That would be safest."

Her mouth made a little O of horror. "Oh, Isaak. So you have inherited your father's curse."

"And only Rapunzel can save me." The words were out of his mouth before he'd thought about them. He wasn't even sure if he believed them. Believed that anyone could save him. "She thinks my heart will give out, just as his did, if she cannot break the curse."

"May I?" she asked.

He shrugged. "Can I stop you? I would caution you not to touch me. I believe I must touch things with my hands for them to turn to gold, but I would hate for you to meet the same fate as the late king of Flamand did at my father's hands before he died."

"A kindness, I am sure," Zuleika said, before she closed her eyes. She bit her lip, frowning. "There is magic in you. It runs through your blood, just as mine does, but I can harness mine to do my bidding, while yours…resists even my efforts to make it do anything. You will be pleased to know that your heart appears to be as healthy as my own, or my husband's, so it is unlikely that it will kill you any time soon."

That came as a relief. Perhaps the curse had not had time to harm him yet.

"Just out of interest, how do you get into the tower? There is no door, and I don't imagine you can cast a portal, as I can," Zuleika said.

Isaak stretched out his legs and pointed at his boots. He hadn't yet bothered to change into a pair of ordinary ones. Or perhaps he hoped the witch would depart soon, so that he might spend another night in Rapunzel's bed. Or every night.

"Are those Dalia's boots? They were made for her by the royal shoemaker in Kasmirus as a gift. She enchanted them so that they might grant her entrance to anywhere she wished. How did you come to possess such a wonder?"

"Queen Molina gave them to me. She said they belonged to my father."

Zuleika nodded slowly. "So my grandmother knew your father. I did not know that. I wonder if she foresaw what he would use them for."

"Whatever he did, all he wanted was to save me," Isaak said. He knew that now, though he wasn't sure what he felt about it. Would he have wanted his father to commit treason to save his life? Not that his father had given him the choice, for he'd been too young to understand, let alone choose.

"I'm sure he did. We are all willing to go to great lengths for the people we love."

Zuleika seemed lost in a memory, her eyes unfocussed, while Isaak's gaze arrowed straight up to the tower. Where there was no flag in sight.

Did he love Rapunzel? Would he commit treason for her?

Perhaps not yet, but he feared it would not take long before he would.

King Lubos himself had given her away to a witch to protect her. Could Isaak steal her away from a witch for the same reason?

Zuleika rose to her feet. "Do you remember my name, young Rumpelstiltskin?"

Isaak nodded. "I do."

"I feel a desire to help you with your quest to save the princess. When you find yourself in need of my assistance, call for me. I shall come." She placed her index finger between her teeth and bit down. Then she traced a circle in the air with her finger, and a portal opened. Not dark, like the ones made by his boots, but one made of pure light. She stepped through. "I shall see you again soon, Isaak," she said, as the portal closed behind her.

Twenty-Two

"I don't know what's more stubborn – a Viken, or a Southern Islander. Put them both together and you get King Rudolf and his fiery sow of a bride, a pair so happy with everything they have they have no desire to conquer anything beyond their own kingdom. A Viken who does not want to raid! He must have been knocked over the head one too many times in battle," Kun grumbled as she stomped down the stairs to the kitchen.

Rapunzel had removed all evidence of Isaak's visit, so now she set a place for Kun across from her own. "Do you wish them to die slowly and painfully, too, Mother?" Rapunzel asked.

Kun sighed. "No. Let the fools enjoy their happiness while it lasts. Heaven knows it took Briska long enough to bring them together. I shall simply look elsewhere for assistance. Rudolf's cousin is king of Viken. Surely he will see the need to conquer the world, and as Rudolf has vowed fealty to him, where one goes, the other will follow. Someone must see reason…"

"So you don't need me any more?" Rapunzel ventured.

Kun laughed. "Of course I need you, child. Perhaps not tonight, but if Reidar sees reason, then I will need you to map out his campaigns, and see that he is successful in his conquests. No one else can weave the future like you. If we are to change the world, we must do it together." She kissed Rapunzel's cheek, then picked up her bowl and headed for the stove to serve herself.

"Have you ever cast a spell you wished to undo?" Rapunzel asked, before she could stop herself. "I mean, like if you punished someone who had learned their lesson, or if the spell hurt someone else it was not supposed to, or something like that." She dared not be too specific.

Slowly, Kun lowered her chopsticks. "Have I made a mistake, you mean? I'm sure I might have made one or two. Mostly being too lenient instead of too harsh, but everything worked out all right in the end. For men rarely learn their lesson, and if you stop punishing them too soon, they only go back to their bad old ways, and you have to start over. No, I usually give them a way to break the curse that is so damned near impossible, they usually choose to live with it rather than go to all the trouble of breaking it."

Like insisting on her cat being brought back to life. Something Rapunzel still didn't know how to do.

"But didn't you make a mistake with King Thorn and Lady Zuleika?" Rapunzel ventured.

"It was Briska, not I, who made the mistake, though it might have turned out well had Zuleika not been so clever." Kun sighed. "She would have made a far more useful djinn than Briska. The power that girl has, at my disposal…I might not have needed Briska or even you if I'd had her." She looked wistful. "But she is too canny. She will never help me. Instead, she hares off on schemes of her own, not realising that I have been playing politics since long before she was born."

"But if you asked her, maybe explained what you're doing and why…surely she would see the logic in working with you. In helping you, as I do. Wouldn't she, Mother?"

"Perhaps," Kun allowed. "But only if she has not gone soft with motherhood, thinking only of her own brood and no further than her own insignificant borders."

That was the answer, then. If Rapunzel

wanted to be free to go with Isaak, to find a way to break his curse, she would have to persuade Zuleika and perhaps other, more powerful magic practitioners to join Kun in her crusade.

"What about the man who killed your cat? I forget his name," Rapunzel said.

"The dying knight? He was a fool, if ever I met one. He came to me to beg me to help his family, and he was so intent on his quest he didn't even notice my poor cat. No, he deserved everything that came to him, and so did his descendants. The family has untold riches stashed away in that castle of theirs, as a result of the curse he asked me to cast. If some of their sons die young, what of it? It is the women who keep a family together, who defend the castle while the men are off playing at war. One of his many times great-grandsons tried to steal you from your mother. I keep you safe in this tower from him even now. If anyone deserves to be cursed, it's men like that. Men who think girls can be bartered and sold, like they are nothing but a sack of rice, instead of people with intellect far superior to their own. They deserve to die out, before they can breed. I'm surprised the bloodline survived for as long as it has."

Rapunzel slumped in her seat. Kun would never take the curse away from Isaak – even if she did manage to bring the cat back to life. She would have to find another way.

But if she could find someone to help Kun in her place…perhaps she'd be allowed to leave the tower to try.

Yes, that's what she would do. As soon as Kun departed for Viken, she would ask Isaak for his help.

Twenty-Three

When the sun rose the next morning, Isaak could barely believe his eyes – Rapunzel's gown fluttered from the window again, as rosy as the early morning light.

After he'd taken her on the kitchen table, and up against the wall, and several times in her bed, she confessed she'd devised a plan to get the witch to let her go.

"But it will only work if we have several powerful allies on our side," Rapunzel said.

"Princess Zuleika the enchantress, for one. And Amani the sorcerer, too, if we can. Now, if we could convince Master Zoticus, the deadliest assassin in the world to help, that would truly be a coup. You would have to visit all three of them, and convince them to travel here to offer Kun their support for her cause. It would not be easy, for they are probably three of the most powerful people in the world, after Kun, of course."

"And leave you here alone as the witch's prisoner? Never!" Isaak said, stroking her thigh and wishing he could take his gloves off so he might feel if her skin was as silken as it appeared. One day, he promised himself, if she could break the curse. On that day, he would stroke her all over, before making love to her.

"You must," Rapunzel insisted. "Without their help, she will never let me leave. Besides, Kun would never hurt me. She keeps me here to protect me. She wishes me to call her Mother, as though I were a child of her own blood instead of just one of likely dozens, if not hundreds, of godchildren.”

Isaak sighed. “Very well. I will find them, and I will win them to your cause, and I shall bring them here. Then, I will take you home with me to Flamand.”

“And while you are gone, I will continue to try to find a way to break the curse,” Rapunzel promised.

“But I will not depart until the morning, and we still have the rest of the day and all night…” Isaak began, parting her thighs.

Her eyes shone, begging him for what he knew they both wanted.

So of course he gave it to her, until she screamed his name to the heavens, and Isaak wished the night would never end.

Twenty-Four

Isaak waited until he'd gone through the garden gates before he dared to call Lady Zuleika's name.

It was quite a while before she answered, and she seemed distracted when she appeared, with half the lacings down the front of her dress hanging loose. Perhaps he and Rapunzel were not the only ones who'd been engaged in vigorous bed play. Isaak hid a smile.

Zuleika yawned. "Sorry it took me so long.

My son needed feeding, and he will not stop until he has drunk every drop." She glanced down, suddenly realising the state of her dress, and in a moment everything was as tightly laced as any court lady's gown. "He will be King of Aros one day, on his uncle's death, but that is a long way off yet. I hope he has learned to drink ale instead of milk by the time the crown passes to him." She blinked and straightened. "Now, what was it you needed my help with?"

Isaak explained Rapunzel's plan.

Zuleika looked doubtful at first, but when Isaak mentioned the names of the other people Rapunzel wished him to recruit, she clapped her hands. "Oh, excellent! We will start with Zoticus. My uncle is always interested in playing at politics."

Isaak choked. "Your uncle is the deadliest assassin in the world?"

Zuleika narrowed her eyes. "Who told you that?"

Isaak swallowed. If he didn't tell her, would

she magic the answer out of him against his will? Probably. Finally, he said, "Rapunzel. The lost princess."

Zuleika nodded. "How she would know that, locked in her tower, I have no idea. He would say he has a reputation, but whether it was deserved or not, he would only shrug. No one knows how many people he has killed, for no one can actually name someone who has died at his hand. And yet…he has such a fearsome reputation, that surely he earned somehow…" She shook her head. "It does not matter. He is always a good man to have at one's side when confronting someone powerful, so we will visit him first." She bit her finger, then traced a circle in the air. Halfway through the portal, she held out her hand. "Are you coming?"

He clasped her hand in his glove and followed.

More mountains and more trees, even if they were different. These mountains had more snow on them, and the trees were chestnuts, not peaches. But it was the lake stretched out as far as he could see, reflecting the sky like an enormous mirror, that he could not take his eyes away from.

"Mirroten," Zuleika said, gesturing toward the village clustered on the lake shore. "They named it after the lake." She led the way up the road, past the mill and the church, until she stopped at what appeared to be the grandest house in town. Of course an assassin would be able to afford the best house. Death did not come cheaply. "Don't look like that. The house belongs to his wife. She owns a castle stronghold further up in the mountains, too. That's how they survived the plague, when it came to their town – they hid behind the walls, where it couldn't reach them." She rapped on the door.

A grey-haired woman answered it. "Yes?"

"We've come to see Zoticus, Aunt Sara," Zuleika said.

The woman blinked. "You're Zoticus's niece?"

Zuleika bobbed her head. "Yes, the youngest one. Zuleika. I'm also Rossa's godmother."

"I thought you'd be older. Well, come in. Rossa and Boris have come to visit, so he's out in the woods with them. He'll be back before dark, I'm sure." She beckoned them inside.

Isaak had eaten so much cake and drunk so much sweet cider, he feared he'd burst, by the time he heard the others returning. Lady Sara – for that's what her maids called her when they brought in another jug of cider or came to ask her about dinner – had chatted with Zuleika about trade in the region, which Sara was surprisingly knowledgeable about. For a woman who lived in such a tiny village…did all of these people possess magic mirrors like Rapunzel?

When Sara rose to greet her family, Zuleika leaned closer to Isaak and said, "Don't look so shocked. Lady Sara owns most of the land from the mountains to the sea, and all along the river almost to Rialto. She's ruled these lands since she was younger than we are. She likes it here, because this is where she grew up, so this is her home. And for any man who thinks to try to take any of her lands from her…well, there's Zoticus."

The grizzled old man who entered the room didn't look dangerous. Oh, he moved fluidly, like he'd had plenty of fighting training, but he barely even blinked to see strangers sitting at his table. Or one stranger, for he kissed Zuleika on both cheeks before embracing her.

Behind him was a man who Isaak might have mistaken for a bear. And lastly came a dark-haired girl he recognised.

"The necromancer!" he blurted out.

All three froze.

Then the old man turned to the girl. "You never told me you could do that."

She shrugged. "I only animated a squirrel once for a training exercise, when you weren't home to train with me. It wasn't that big a deal. It's not like I was going around a battlefield, raising all the corpses into an army to conquer the world."

The old man grinned. "But you could. If you wanted to."

The girl pouted. "Maybe. I can't imagine ever wanting to, though."

The old man turned to the bear man. "When she's your queen, you remember that. You'll never lose a battle with her at your side."

The bear man grunted. "We never lose a battle now."

The old man looked outraged. "You take my only daughter into battle?"

The bear man met the old assassin's gaze without flinching. "You try keeping her out of a fight she wants to win."

The old man just laughed, before he sobered and turned his gaze on Isaak. A moment of that implacable stare and Isaak was ready to drop to his knees and tell the man anything he wanted. How had the bear man withstood it?

"So, strange boy who knows my daughter's

secrets. What are you doing here?"

Isaak told him everything. From Rapunzel to Abraham to Molina and how he'd come here with Zuleika. Then he pulled off one of his gloves and reached for the nearest cider cup.

"Well, isn't that a nice trick," Zoticus drawled, for the old man could be no one else.

Isaak put his glove back on. "It's a terrible curse, my lord, and I have come to beg your help to free the only person who might be able to break it. I can pay you with as much gold as you desire, but I beg you…"

Zoticus waved him into silence. "I get bored with begging, boy. And I have no need for gold, cursed or otherwise. But a witch who wants to remake the world, now that is something I might need to see." He exchanged a glance with Zuleika, who bit her lip and nodded. "I will come with you to this tower."

Rossa and the bear man exchanged a glance of their own. "So shall we," she said.

Isaak wasn't sure whether to worry or

rejoice. So… "Thank you," he said, hoping it would suffice.

"Don't thank me yet, boy. Wherever these two go, trouble usually follows. And I have a premonition this will not go as smoothly as you hope it will," Zoticus said, reaching for the golden cup. "After all, Sara hasn't seen what you've done to her favourite cup."

Twenty-Five

They left Zoticus and his family in their house by the lake, promising to come for them on the morrow.

"Where to next?" Isaak asked.

Zuleika frowned. "To Amani's desert palace. You'd better pray he's home and answering the gate, for if he isn't he could be anywhere, and we might travel the whole world over and not find him, if he does not want to be found. And remember, he calls himself a sorcerer. The most powerful sorcerer in the world, and he's not lying."

"What's the difference between a sorcerer and a witch?" Isaak asked.

Zuleika shrugged. "Truly? Nothing. His magic works the same way as mine or Rossa's or Zoticus's, but he just calls it by a different name. I suppose I'm just as bad, calling myself an enchantress instead of a common witch, but there are few people who inherited as much magic as I did, and everyone called my mother an enchantress. I suppose that would make Amani an enchanter, if his power is equal to mine. The last time we met, I…may have bested him in a fight, though, and he might still be a little sore about it. If he remembers."

"I'll never forget the last time a girl bested me in a fight," Isaak said glumly. "He's going to take one look at you and kick us clean across the desert for sure."

"Not necessarily. He was a djinn the last time we met. The binding messes with your mind. Make you more docile. A slave, really, in the worst possible way, because the spell doesn't just bind your body, but your mind as well. You're forced to obey, and you feel like you want to. It's a terrible fate that I wouldn't wish upon anyone. A djinn's master could force them to do terrible things, which they would do their best to forget so they don't go mad. He managed to get free, so his mind must have remained intact, somehow. The best we can hope for is that he doesn't remember me at all."

So when they arrived at the gates of the massive palace perched amid an ocean of sand dunes, it was Isaak who knocked.

An enormous blue man, wearing nothing but a loincloth that barely covered the essentials, appeared before the gate. "What business do you have with my master, the mighty sorcerer, Lord Amani?" the man boomed.

Isaak blinked. Was it his imagination, or could he see through the man? Like he was made of blue mist or fog or…

Zuleika stepped up to Isaak's side. "We're here to offer vengeance to Amani, on the witch who parted him from his beloved."

The apparition seemed to jump. "You!"

Zuleika nodded grimly. "Me."

"What did you do to the foolish prince after you forced his rogue djinn back into his lamp?" the apparition demanded.

Zuleika grinned. "I turned him into a frog, and in order to break the curse, I made it so that he had to persuade a girl to sleep with him, slimy skin and all. All night, too."

The apparition grinned. "So he will be a frog forever, then! Ah, you must come inside and toast his fate with my master." He swung the gates wide, and bowed so low his forehead touched the sand.

Zuleika and Isaak followed the blazing hot path into the much cooler confines of the palace. But when Isaak turned to see what had happened to the apparition, he found it had vanished.

Inside the palace, they were greeted by a

man who looked like a smaller version of the apparition, only he wasn't blue. "The young enchantress, and your companion. You are welcome in my home."

Zuleika folded her arms across her chest. "You're the last man I ever expected would employ a djinn as a servant."

The man grinned, waving his hands wildly. "No, no! He was no djinn. Merely a phantasm, made in my own image from when I was a djinn. Did you like him? He answers the gate, frightening away any travellers who do not belong here, but if anyone does have business with me…I can speak through the phantasm instead of having to walk all the way to the gate. Ingenious, no?"

"Lazy, too," Zuleika said.

"Of course! But if you lived in the desert heat as I do, you would avoid it as much as you can, too. Come, I have refreshments prepared. You must come and drink and tell me about the trials and tribulations of the frog prince!"

"Actually, Isaak here wants to tell you about a witch who wants to remake the world, one royal court at a time. Matching those with magical gifts, or wealth, or lands, or power, to keep them all in the hands of the people she chooses. Enslaving a queen to matchmake young royals to better breed more magic into their bloodlines. Capturing a princess and who knows how many more to help her in her unholy quest..."

The man's eyes had gone entirely black.

Isaak shivered.

"Mistress Kun," the man said. "You know where she is?"

Zuleika nodded. "Isaak found her home. The secret tower, hidden in the mountains far to the east, where she keeps a princess captive, bound to a magic mirror..."

"Let me at her and I will tear her limbs off, one by one!" the man roared.

Isaak backed up, hands up to placate the madman. This wasn't the sort of ally Rapunzel had meant. She wanted someone who would help the witch, not kill her.

But Zuleika didn't seem to care. "We're headed there in the morning," she drawled. "Care to meet us there?"

"A thousand wild camels could not drag me away," the man promised.

"Nor me," Zuleika said cheerfully. "See you in the morning, then, Amani."

Then she cast another portal, and pulled Isaak through after her. It wasn't until the portal had closed that he dared to ask, "Are you mad? He wants to kill the witch!"

Zuleika just shook her head. "The witch who holds your princess captive enslaved Amani's wife for almost twenty years, forcing her to do all manner of terrible things to people. A quick death at Amani's hands is probably better than she deserves for just the crimes we know about. If you want to persuade the witch to release your princess, you will need both him and Zoticus to remind her of what will happen if she doesn't."

Isaak felt the blood drain from his face. "So

of the three of you, you're the only ally I'm actually bringing with me?"

Zuleika bared her teeth so fiercely Isaak took a step back. "I will rip that woman's still beating heart out of her chest if she so much as thinks about subjecting someone else to the same thing she made Briska do to me. I would rather die than ally with that heartless bitch. The poor, naïve girl sent you out in search of allies. You have us – with more magic and power between us than most of the rest of the population. We stand with you. We will free the captive princess. And we will annihilate anyone who thinks to treat our world, and all the people in it, like their plaything."

"And my curse?" he whispered, half hoping she hadn't heard him.

She shrugged. "I have a good track record with breaking some really bad ones. With help from the others, I'll give it my best shot."

Well, that was something, at least. If the most magical people in the world were willing to help him, could he truly ask for more?

Twenty-Six

They slept in Lady Sara's house, where she made sure they'd eaten a hearty breakfast before sending them off to save the world, or that's what she called it. She did not seem the slightest bit worried about her husband or her daughter going off to visit a witch half a world away.

Zoticus seemed to have read Isaak's thoughts, for he said, "My sister battled dragons and won, but my wife could persuade them to wash their claws and use their best manners as they sat down at her table. If Lady Sara wanted to remake the world, I would bring it to her on a platter, and marvel at the results. And she, sweet lady that she is, would deny having done anything. For the world would have rearranged itself just to please her."

"Is Lady Sara a witch?" Isaak asked as they stepped thought the portal, and he found himself outside Kun's garden gates. "Because I don't know what you'd call that sort of magic, but it sure sounds powerful."

"What does it do?"

Isaak couldn't help but stare at the most beautiful woman he'd ever laid eyes on. Every curve was perfect, from the bottom of her slippered foot to the bow of the impossibly long, dark lashes fringing her equally dark eyes. He opened his mouth, but only incoherent sounds seemed able to come out.

"Princess Maram! It has been so long!" Zoticus surged forward, and enveloped the beauty in a hug.

All of a sudden, she looked awkward instead of graceful, as if she wanted to bolt in three different directions at once.

The spell that had overcome Isaak released him. She was still a beautiful woman, but he no longer felt the urge to prostrate himself before her. Only now did he see the two men who flanked her, almost like bodyguards.

But even they didn't dare lay hands on Zoticus.

"Lady Sara has less magic than the swans that float on her lake. Whereas Princess Maram here can cast a charm spell so powerful, no one is immune to it," Zoticus said.

Maram coughed delicately. "With one exception. My husband, Aladdin, and his friend, Kaveh." She gestured to the men on her right and left.

"And when your magic goes awry, there is always poison, which I am only too happy to supply!" Zoticus continued.

Maram ducked her head, suddenly obsessed with the toes of her silk slippers. "He deserved it," she whispered.

Her husband and his friend nodded vigorously.

"That he did," Amani said. "I felt that Maram's expertise with djinn might come in useful. Of course, her husband and his friend wanted to come, too, so I brought them along. They, too, have experience with djinn."

From the glances exchanged between the three men, Isaak saw secrets he wasn't sure he wanted to know.

"Whereas my daughter and her friend came along to keep a frail old man out of trouble," Zoticus said cheerfully.

The bear man, whose name was Boris, Isaak had learned, grunted, "You are trouble, old man."

Zuleika stepped forward, making introductions, so everyone knew everyone's names.

When she introduced herself, Maram

flushed. "You are…the new Mistress of Beacon Isle?"

"Yes," Zuleika said.

"I hope you like the wedding gift we bestowed upon your husband, some years back. Was his performance…magical?"

Zuleika's mouth dropped open in shock. After a long moment, she managed to say, "Yes, yes, thank you," before putting as much space between herself and Maram as possible.

Then it was Isaak's turn to open a portal through the wall, and lead everyone up to the tower.

He soon found Maram walking beside him, "I cast a pleasure enchantment on her husband's manhood," she said. "Amani tells me you plan to woo a princess. As most of those come in a dozen shades of virginal and shy, I will offer you the same courtesy, if you wish. It will make things go so much more smoothly on your wedding night."

As if Molina and Lubos would ever let him marry their daughter.

Isaak managed to thank Maram for her kind offer, even as he shook his head.

She only gave an expressive shrug. "The offer is still there, if you change your mind!" She skipped off to link her arm with her husband's.

Finally, after a walk that seemed a lot longer than the first time he'd come this way, they reached the foot of the tower.

Twenty-Seven

Isaak opened a portal in the store room and crept upstairs. He found Rapunzel in the kitchen, her face lighting up at the sight of him.

"Isaak!" She flew across the room to kiss him.

"Is she here?" he asked. "The witch?"

"No, but I expect her very soon. She said she'd be back for dinner."

"Good," Isaak said, then called down the

stairs, "You can come up."

The others trooped up into the kitchen, until the place was rather crowded. Rapunzel's eyes widened with each new person who appeared, but as she mouthed each of their names, Isaak didn't think introductions would be necessary.

"Where is she?" Amani asked.

"In…she went to the capital, in Viken," Rapunzel said.

"Where does she cast her portals?"

Rapunzel pointed upward. "In her chamber, on the floor above."

The others trooped up the stairs, with Rapunzel and Isaak bringing up the rear.

"How did you find so many people so quickly?" Rapunzel whispered.

Isaak wasn't sure how to tell her that the woman who'd raised her had far too many enemies, from a lifetime of terrible deeds. It was worse than learning that his father had been a traitor. He'd never thought his father was a saint, whereas Rapunzel…

She wouldn't forgive him for this. Unless he hung back, and took no part in it. Yes, it might brand him a coward, but there was a lot of magic in those people, and when the spells started flying, he and Rapunzel were probably the weakest people present. The best he could do was throw his body over hers and try to shield her from it all.

Only when he reached the witch's bedchamber, everyone stood shoulder to shoulder against the walls, so that there was no way he or Rapunzel could enter the room at all.

"Isaak, what are they doing?" Rapunzel asked urgently.

He wrapped his arms around her. "I don't know."

Twenty-Eight

A blinding flash of light appeared in the middle of the room, and Rapunzel was too dazzled to see. But she could hear Kun's voice, and she wasn't happy.

"Damned Viken and their thrice-damned harpy queen! Why didn't the dragon eat her, like it did her sisters? She's the king of Kasmirus's only remaining daughter, the heir to the throne, and neither she nor her husband want to conquer Kasmirus, to seize it from the dragonslaying shoemaker and his seamstress bride, when they're her goddamned birthright!"

The shrieks turned even more shrill, until suddenly, they fell silent.

The crowd shuffled away, back toward the walls. All but the biggest man among them, who was crouched over Kun, who lay crumpled on the floor.

"Oh no," someone said.

The man lifted his paw – for his entire arm was furred and clawed like it belonged to a bear and not a man – and blood dripped from it. "That is for my wife and daughter," he spat.

The girl in red – Rossa – grabbed his human arm and hauled him to his feet, away from Kun.

Only then did Rapunzel rush to her side.

But she was too late.

Glassy eyes stared at the ceiling, above a throat that had been torn out. Blood pooled on the floor, just as it had after Thorn's cowardly attack.

"No more women will be raped or killed on her orders. Never again," the bear man said. He must be Boris, the bear who never left Rossa's side.

"No, no, Mother, this is terrible. Someone get me a pillow for her head," Rapunzel snapped.

She felt someone tugging at her arm, trying to pull her to her feet, away from Kun, but Rapunzel would not be moved.

"A pillow, now!" she cried.

It came, and she lifted Kun's head on her floppy neck to slide the pillow between her and the cold flagstones.

"She's dead, child. There's nothing more you can do for her," someone said gently.

Rapunzel glared at them all. "She is not dead, and the healing process will take days, seeing as she's lost so much blood. I'll have to clean the floor, and her body, and her clothes, and all before she wakes up. And when she does, she'll want to do the most terrible things to all of you. I'll try to make her forget, or lessen the curses, but she won't forgive something like this. Even Thorn ran her through in his court, but you invaded her home. The one place we were safe."

"You're safe now she's gone. Go with young Isaak there. He'll take you to Flamand where you can be reunited with your family."

Rapunzel wanted to punch something. "Kun is my family! She raised me and kept me safe and as soon as she recovers, she will again!"

"But she's dead, child."

"No, she isn't!" Rapunzel seized Kun's hand, where her ring still glowed blue. "As long as this light shines, she still lives. She told me that herself, the first time I thought she'd died."

A man Rapunzel didn't recognise stepped forward. "She's a djinn," he said. "She's not dead because she's a djinn."

"That's not…"

"She can't be!"

"She's the only one who can bind djinn, she

can't possibly be one!"

"Take the ring!"

"Break the binding!"

"NO!" Rapunzel shouted, ripping the ring off Kun's finger and slipping it onto her own. "Heal," she begged her godmother. These people did not have the right to decide her fate. Kun deserved a say in it, too.

Everyone closed in, reaching for her, until Isaak was there, lifting her up in his arms. "Anyone touches her or me, and I'll turn you to gold."

Suddenly there was space, as everyone shuffled to put as much distance between themselves and Isaak as possible.

But still they were arguing, not believing her even as the ring on her finger glowed and the hole in Kun's throat was closing. She needed to distract them and convince them all at once.

Rapunzel closed her eyes. "Do you want to know her story? What her king did to her, before she won her freedom? I'll show you. Mirror, show them the first time Kun came to the garden."

She did not need to look. She would never forget the heartbreaking look on Kun's dying mother's face as she begged the girl – for she had only been a girl – not to go on such a dangerous quest to the king's garden. The king would never allow her one of the peaches of immortality, the fruit that could heal every illness. But Kun had not listened, and she'd refused to even say farewell to her mother, for she meant to come back with a peach.

Kun climbed the garden walls, cutting her clothes and her shins to ribbons on the rough stone, but she didn't give up until she stood in the king's garden. She made her way to the peach orchard, and plucked one perfect fruit…only to be caught by the king himself, who declared her theft treason, for it was treason to steal from the king. But when the king would have killed her, she summoned all the powers within her to throw a rock at the king. Her magic was what had both doomed and saved her, for instead of killing her, the king had bound her to one of his rings, and forced her to serve him. Not for a normal lifetime, but for centuries, for the peaches kept him young.

Until one day, he slipped on the stairs and broke his neck. A peach still might have saved him, but it was Kun who found him, and instead of helping the man who'd enslaved her for all those years, she took the ring from his finger, as the light died in his eyes.

She claimed the garden and its peach trees for her own. And she'd taken a whole basket full of them home…only to find that not only her mother, but her whole village was gone, swept away by floods years before.

So she took to protecting her own children, and their children, helping those who called upon her, becoming a fairy godmother to all of her descendants. Until there were enough magically talented people in the world to take over that task for her, and she wandered the world, helping some and ending the reigns of others.

And she was still doing it, even today, trying to persuade the Viken king to do what was right for the world, for her descendants.

Heal, Rapunzel begged Kun silently, while the others watched the mirror. Because no one could plead Kun's case better than Kun herself. They had to help her.

Finally, the wound in Kun's throat closed, and she began to breathe again.

Twenty-Nine

"We need to break the binding and kill her, before she wakes up."

"But she was just a girl. A child. She might look like an old woman now, but she's still just a child who didn't know any better."

"How many people has she wrongfully enslaved, or hurt, or killed, all in the name of her crusade for a world like she wants? If we let her wake up, she'll never stop. This needs to end here. Now."

"But you can't just kill her. Everyone deserves a fair trial."

"We need to break the binding. Whatever she has done, she deserves to be free."

Everyone fell silent and stared at Maram. "We need to find someone who carries the blood of the king who bound her."

"That was centuries ago!"

"There's no way…"

"Impossible!"

Rapunzel cleared her throat. "Actually, we all do. Everyone except Kun, because we're all descendants of her time serving the king."

Zuleika and Boris looked stricken. Maram and Rossa looked like they might be sick.

"She served him for centuries," Amani said softly. "How many children did she bear him?"

"I don't know," Rapunzel said. "I couldn't keep track of them all. I'm not sure even she could, but I do know that she could trace them through the magic in their bloodlines. Every child who could use their magic was one of her descendants, or the king's descendants. So any of us, or all of us, could use the magic in our blood to break the binding, and free her." She swallowed. "But we must do it now that she is healed, before she wakes."

In the end, they all gave a drop of blood, just in case, and Maram cast the spell, for she had released djinn before.

All eyes fixed on the ring as Maram said the words, waiting, watching.

The glow died. A ragged cheer went up.

And on the floor, Kun let out a terrible groan.

Maram bit her lip, and flicked her fingers toward Kun, who subsided, and started to snore.

"It's just a sleep spell," she said.

They all stared at Kun, who'd transformed from an old woman back into a young girl. No one seemed as eager to hurt her now.

"When she wakes up, she'll still remember everything," the man beside Maram said. "A djinn with a master might forget, but a djinn who is their own master remembers everything."

"So, she must forget. Forget all about her family, and her enslavement with the king, and everything since, so she's just a girl who doesn't remember anything," Zuleika said. She glanced around. "Anyone here know how to erase centuries of memories with a single spell without destroying her mind?"

They all shook their heads.

"A few memories, I might manage, but not everything," Amani said.

Rapunzel closed her eyes. She did not wish to hurt Kun, who had cared for her all her life, but the others would punish her for her crimes if she did not do this. She took a deep breath. "I know a way to make her forget. But it will be permanent. From the moment the spell is finished, she will not remember a thing. She will be like any other girl of her age, with no memories."

"What do you need?" Zuleika asked.

"First, I need you all to promise that once the spell is complete, you will never seek to remind her, or punish her for the past," Rapunzel said.

Grudgingly, they all muttered some sort of promise to that effect. Even if they were lying, they had given their consent. That was all she needed.

"Then I will need a lock of hair from everyone, including Kun."

Someone found some scissors, and they began snipping. When Maram offered to cut Rapunzel's hair for her, she shook her head. "My hair is already the warp behind the spell. Yours will form the image on the tapestry — the future we want to create, where Kun forgets."

Finally, she had hair from everyone.

"Now, see that she stays asleep, and I will come down when I am done," Rapunzel said, climbing the stairs to her workroom.

Thirty

Only a small tapestry today, Rapunzel told herself as she cut a lock of her own hair and threaded it along the loom. Next, she dug out her basket of silks, and laid each lock of hair on the table.

She worked fast, weaving a little from each lock into the cloth, then returning to see the picture taking shape. Everyone needed to be in it, as everyone's hair formed a part of it.

Normally, she stopped to eat and drink and

sleep, but this time, Rapunzel knew Kun's life depended on her doing this quickly. She owed her this much.

Perhaps the figures on the tapestry were not as clear as they could have been. But she could make out Kun's dark hair, along with Rossa's and Maram's and Zuleika's, though all four wore different coloured gowns. Aladdin and the other man who stayed close to Maram were indistinguishable from one another in the picture, but it didn't matter. They were there. Zoticus's silver hair seemed to glimmer in the candlelight, while Boris's was almost indistinguishable from the cloth, it was so pale. Lastly, Isaak's gold hair stood out in the centre, for that's where he was to her – front and centre in all of this. He'd handed the hair to her with his gloved hand, so as not to hurt her. If only she could break his curse as easily as they'd freed Kun from her djinn binding.

If she could only allow Kun to wake, and try to persuade her to save Isaak…but Rapunzel knew she would never agree.

So she resolved to ask Rossa the necromancer to cast her reanimation spell on the cat's corpse, in the hope that it would be enough to break the curse.

She had to hope.

She'd woven everyone's hair into the tapestry, but still she had a clump of Isaak's sitting on the table. That would not do. She'd done his hair, and his golden breastplate. Then she had a silly idea.

Well, why not?

Some time later, she laid the tapestry on the table. All of them were in it, clustered around a radiantly armoured Isaak, and in his arms, he carried a golden-yellow cat.

Thirty-One

Wearier than she could ever remember being before, Rapunzel stumbled down the steps to Kun's chamber. The girl's eyes fluttered, and she looked straight at Rapunzel.

"Where am I? Who are you?" she asked.

Rapunzel smiled gently. The spell had worked. "An evil wizard took you prisoner, but you're safe now," she said. "Would you like to come downstairs with me to get something to eat?"

The girl nodded, and slid out of bed. She followed Rapunzel.

Everyone else was clustered in the kitchen, waiting for something.

But no one seemed to remember what.

"She's awake," Rapunzel said, as all eyes turned to young Kun.

Her own eyes widened. "Which one is the evil wizard?" she asked.

"None of them. All of them saved you from the evil wizard," Rapunzel said.

Confusion reigned for a moment, before they seemed to accept it. They were, after all, the sort of people who prided themselves on saving innocent girls from evil wizards.

"Shall I make us something to eat, before we all head home?" Rapunzel said. She headed for the stove before anyone answered, knowing that even if they all chose not to eat with her, she was hungry, and she might as well make enough for everyone.

"Do you have any fish? I, for one, am starving," said a new voice Rapunzel didn't recognise.

She turned and couldn't help but stare as a large, yellow cat leaped onto the table, wearing Isaak's black boots.

"And who are you?" she asked the cat, reaching out to stroke its fur.

The cat struck a most uncatlike pose. "I, fair maiden, am Sir Kempenich von Rumpelstiltskin, at your service. I would lay my sword at your feet, but it seems to have gone missing." He glared around the table, as though he suspected someone of stealing it.

"Come on," Isaak said, reaching for the strange creature. "Cats off the table." He grabbed it with his bare hands and set it down on the floor.

The cat sniffed and sauntered off, looking very put out.

Thirty-Two

After they'd eaten, they got up to say their farewells. Amani and Maram had offered to take young Kun to Briska, as she was probably the best suited of all of them to mother a teenage girl with magic powers. In Amani's desert palace, far from everyone else, they could keep her from causing any magical mishaps until she had her powers under control.

They all agreed to answer the others' calls if

they had need of them – the evil wizard might be gone, but a new threat might arise, and together, they would be stronger, and more able to take it down.

Finally, only Isaak and Rapunzel were left in the tower. Zuleika and Amani had offered to cast a portal for them to take them home to Flamand, but they'd both refused.

"This will probably sound terrible, but I've forgotten your name," Isaak said when everyone else was gone.

She'd smiled, and opened her mouth to tell him the name she'd always known, for she'd been named after the plant her father had bargained with the witch for.

But she'd had another name, one she'd nearly forgotten, and only when she looked in the mirror did she remember what it was.

"I'm Tessarina, but you can call me Tessa," she said.

He took her hands in his. His hands were rough and calloused, and she wondered what he'd worked so hard at to make them that way.

"I'm Isaak, in case I forgot to introduce myself."

Tessa laughed softly. "Well, when we first met, I'm not sure names and good manners were uppermost in our minds. I seem to recall tangling together on the store room floor."

His eyes widened. "I remember that! I worried that it was nothing but a dream. Later, did I at least have the courtesy to take you up to your bedchamber, to make love to you properly?"

Tessa nodded. "Several times, before we came down to the kitchen to eat, and make use of the kitchen table."

"Was that when I laid you down on the table, naked, and rubbed oil all over your body as you moaned in ecstasy, before making love to you until you screamed?" he asked hopefully.

Now that was something he'd never done with the other girls back in Flamand. "Maybe you can remind me?" Tessa suggested, finding a bottle of oil. She set it down on the table and began to take off her clothes.

Within moments, he indeed had her moaning, then begging for more. He was every bit as skilful with his hands as she'd dreamed he would be, and then when he leaned down to use his mouth as well…oh, now that was something she would never forget. He devoured her on the kitchen table until she was sopping wet with need, and begging for all that he could give her.

So he lifted her legs over his shoulders, caressing her oiled thighs as he fitted himself between her legs, and thrust deep.

She bucked and clenched around him, wanting to savour this pleasure forever. Making love with Isaak, now mercifully free of the curse, as his hands roamed across her body exactly the way she wanted them too.

And if she screamed until she was hoarse, as her body surrendered to wave after wave of pleasure, entwined with the man she loved, she felt she was allowed, after finding a way to free the two of them from the ties that bound them, so that they might be allowed to live without anyone remembering a past neither of them had chosen.

For all they could choose was the future, and while Tessa had not been able to weave her own future into a tapestry, she wove one now, twining her body with Isaak's, until she did not know where he ended and she began, and she didn't care, for they belonged together, and they deserved happiness just like this.

About the Author

Demelza Carlton has always loved the ocean, but on her first snorkelling trip she found she was afraid of fish.

She has since swum with sea lions, sharks and sea cucumbers and stood on spray drenched cliffs over a seething sea as a seven-metre cyclonic swell surged in, shattering a shipwreck below.

Demelza now lives in Perth, Western Australia, the shark attack capital of the world.

The *Ocean's Gift* series was her first foray into fiction, followed by her suspense thriller *Nightmares* trilogy. She swears the *Mel Goes to Hell* series ambushed her on a crowded train and wouldn't leave her alone.

Want to know more? You can follow Demelza on Facebook, Twitter, YouTube or her website, Demelza Carlton's Place at:

www.demelzacarlton.com

More Books by Demelza Carlton

<u>Colony: Holiday series</u>
Cowboys and Aliens (#1)
Ghost (#2)
Vulcan (#3)
Cupid (#4)
Valentine(#5)
Prometheus (#6)

<u>**Colony: Aqua series**</u>

Halcyon (#1)

Poseidon (#2)

Apollo (#3)

<u>**Colony: Nyx series**</u>

Fang (#1)

Talon (#2)

Claw (#3)

<u>**Siren of Secrets series**</u>

Ocean's Secret (#1)

Ocean's Gift (#2)

Ocean's Infiltrator (#3)

<u>**Siren of War series**</u>

Ocean's Justice (#1)

Ocean's Widow (#2)

Ocean's Bride (#3)

Ocean's Rise (#4)

Ocean's War (#5)

How To Catch Crabs

<u>**Nightmares Trilogy**</u>

Nightmares of Caitlin Lockyer (#1)
Necessary Evil of Nathan Miller (#2)
Afterlife of Alana Miller (#3)

<u>**Mel Goes to Hell series**</u>
The Devil's Work (#1)
See You in Hell (#2)
Mel Goes to Hell (#3)
To Hell and Back (#4)
The Holiday From Hell (#5)
All Hell Breaks Loose (#6)
The Devil Goes to Heaven (#7)

<u>**Romance Island Resort series**</u>
Maid for the Rock Star (#1)
The Rock Star's Email Order Bride (#2)
The Rock Star's Virginity (#3)
The Rock Star and the Billionaire (#4)
The Rock Star Wants A Wife (#5)
The Rock Star's Wedding (#6)
Maid for the South Pole (#7)

Romance a Medieval Fairytale series

Enchant: Beauty and the Beast Retold

Dance: Cinderella Retold

Fly: Goose Girl Retold

Revel: Twelve Dancing Princesses Retold

Silence: Little Mermaid Retold

Awaken: Sleeping Beauty Retold

Embellish: Brave Little Tailor Retold

Appease: Princess and the Pea Retold

Blow: Three Little Pigs Retold

Return: Hansel and Gretel Retold

Wish: Aladdin Retold

Melt: Snow Queen Retold

Spin: Rumpelstiltskin Retold

Kiss: Frog Prince Retold

Reflect: Snow White Retold

Roar: Goldilocks Retold

Cobble: Elves and the Shoemaker Retold

Float: Enchanted Horse Retold

Steal: Forty Thieves Retold

Call: Pied Piper Retold

Fall: Scheherazade Retold

Feather: Swan Maidens Retold

Cross: Billy Goats Gruff Retold

Weave: Rapunzel Retold

Claim: Puss in Boots Retold

Curse: Rose Red Retold

Cross: Three Billy Goats Gruff Retold

Weave: Rapunzel Retold

Claim: Puss in Boots Retold

<u>**Heart of Stone series**</u>

Heart of Steel (#0)

Broken Chains (#1)

Broken Bonds (#2)

Broken Dreams (#3)

www.ingramcontent.com/pod-product-compliance
Lightning Source LLC
Chambersburg PA
CBHW070638170726
48291CB00003B/1058